Bullies
in the
Headlights

OTHER BOOKS AND AUDIO BOOKS
BY MATTHEW BUCKLEY:

Chickens in the Headlights

a novel

Matthew Buckley

Covenant Communications, Inc.

Cover art by Nathan Lindsay

Cover design by Jessica A. Warner © 2007 by Covenant Communications, Inc.

Published by Covenant Communications, Inc.
American Fork, Utah

Copyright © 2007 by Matthew Buckley
All rights reserved. No part of this book may be reproduced in any format or in any medium without the written permission of the publisher, Covenant Communications, Inc., P.O. Box 416, American Fork, UT 84003.

This is a work of fiction. The characters, names, incidents, places, and dialogue are products of the author's imagination, and are not to be construed as real.

Printed in The United States of America
First Printing: May 2007

13 12 11 10 09 08 07   10 9 8 7 6 5 4 3 2 1

ISBN 978-1-59811-326-6

PREFACE

I grew up in a family with ten boys and one girl. I wrote my first book, *Chickens in the Headlights,* because I felt like I had a unique experience. With that large of a family, we had a wild and wonderful childhood, and I wanted to share that childhood with others who didn't have siblings in the double digits. After my book was published, however, I quickly found out that my experiences were far from unique. When I talked to others about my book, they had had similar experiences to those I told in *Chickens.* Families bring a lot of joy, and whether you have a couple of brothers, a single sister, or nine siblings running around, you're in for a good time.

Chickens in the Headlights was based primarily on my childhood. While there were a few sections that were "slightly embellished," for the most part it happened just as I described in the book. This novel is a bit different. Many of the experiences in this book happened, but not in the exact manner described in the book. The Hagbarts are, in fact, entirely fictional. They are based on experiences I had with several bullies while growing up. But the underlying conclusion that Matthew and Simon come to is the same conclusion I eventually came to; I have learned that the best way to deal with those who like to bully is to do exactly as Matthew and Simon do in the book.

After writing *Chickens* I had many readers contact me and tell me funny stories from their childhoods. There were times when I thought, *That story would have fit perfectly in my book!* or, *That's something Matthew would have done!*

It got me thinking . . .

In my line of work I work with "social software." One in particular has captured my interest: the wiki. The most famous wiki is probably Wikipedia. It's an online encyclopedia that is written by . . . everybody. Anybody who is willing can go and edit any entry on the site. It's gotten quite a bit of press, and it works surprisingly well. Though some people like to poke fun at it, a recent study in *Nature* magazine showed that articles from Wikipedia were almost as accurate as those in *Encyclopædia Britannica*. Not bad for a bunch of disorganized amateurs!

I couldn't help but wonder what would happen if a bunch of folks worked together on a piece of fiction. While working on my first book, I quickly found out that it was improved by feedback from others. My wife, my brothers, my editor, my friends—all added to what the book finally became. Sure, it was still "my book," but they all left their imprint, and the book was better because of it.

So, I determined to write my second book (the one you're holding in your hands) in a wiki. As far as I can tell, it's the first work of fiction written that way.

The phrase "if you build it, they will come" works with baseball fields, but not with websites. While working on this book, I had close to a dozen people drop in and make comments. But I'd like many more. So I'd like to extend an invitation to anybody reading this book. I'm working on a third book in the Buckley series. The topic will be Scouting. My father, brothers, and I were all heavily involved with the Scouting program growing up, and have many wild and wonderful stories, but I know that you have even more. If you have any funny, interesting, or crazy Scouting stories, or would like to follow a book as it's written from beginning to end, or if you would like to be involved in any other way, I invite you to swing on by. You can visit my blog at http://chickenarmpits.blogspot.com and click on the "third book" link. That will take you to my wiki, and you can participate in our little experiment. You can find more information about the project on the site.

I would like to thank those that participated in the shaping of this book and signed the wiki: Amber Knowles, Eric Rasmussen, David Wiley, and my brother Robin Jensen. I would especially like to thank my sister-in-law Emily Warburton Jensen, who provided feedback, suggestions, and a whole lot of editing. My parents, Robin and Eleanor Jensen, also had some great suggestions, and several of the scenes in the book became richer due to the memories they shared. I would also like to thank the generous individuals who gave me permission to use their song in my book. The original lyrics on page 62 are by Moiselle Renstrom, used by permission of Jackman Music Corporation, proprietor of its copyright.

I hope you enjoy this book, and, as always, if you have any feedback, I'd love to hear from you at info@covenant-lds.com.

Matthew Buckley

*This book is dedicated to
Jay Macfarlane
and every other Primary teacher I had.
They not only kept us kids in line,
but managed to teach us something at the same time—
a miraculous feat in and of itself.*

PROLOGUE

The deep blue sky, cool breeze, and warm sun that enveloped us should have made it a perfect day—a wonderful day, a day spent playing outdoors with friends or brothers. But instead I had spent a good portion of the day sitting at a desk under dim fluorescent lights and listening to a teacher drone on about the importance of mastering cursive.

But even writing cursive was better than where I was now. I was out on the school grounds, and despite the sun and nice breeze, it was a no-good, rotten, should-have-stayed-in-bed kind of day. The source of the bad day floated serenely against the backdrop of the clear blue sky.

Hanging from the flagpole, right beneath Ol' Glory, was a pair of underpants. Boy's underpants. My underpants. They waved and flapped with gusto, as if to shout, *Look at me! I'm Matthew Buckley's underpants, his Yosemite Sam underpants!*

A hand fell on my shoulder.

"What's going on?"

It was Simon, my brother. Even though he was older than I was, we were about the same height. He had dark hair and thick glasses that he pushed up on his nose so that he could see my now-famous underpants better.

I couldn't say anything or I would surely burst into tears, and that would only compound my shame. I hung my head.

"Who did this?" Simon's voice had taken on a strange edge. He sounded mad.

I shrugged my shoulders.

Simon stood silent for a moment, then took a quick breath. "This was the work of the bullies."

I nodded slowly and quickly flipped up my hand to wipe my eye.

"You know what this means, don't you, Matthew?"

I shook my head.

"It means that the Hagbarts aren't working alone. Bullies as thickheaded as them couldn't come up with a scheme like this."

I looked up at Simon. He was glaring at all the laughing kids. He turned back to me. "You know what else this means, don't you?"

I shook my head again.

"It means we're at war with the bullies."

CHAPTER 1

Don't Forget to Eat the Food on Your Lap

5 Weeks Earlier

"Matthew Buckley! Wake up!"

It seemed a strange thing for a chicken to say. But then again, the chicken was covered in chocolate syrup, about six feet tall, and was eating a small zucchini.

I was trying to kill it with an ax.

"If you don't wake up right now," the chicken said as it suddenly did a backflip, "you're going to miss the first day of school."

The chicken sounded like my mom. I suddenly realized that I wasn't in the backyard chasing a large chicken. I was lying in a nice warm bed. And instead of an ax in my hand, I held my pajama shirt. Somehow I had taken it off in the night, and I now wielded it in my hands before me.

I rubbed my eyes and sat up on the edge of my bed. Mom saw this and moved on to one of my brothers. She grabbed my six-year-old brother Peter by the ankle and physically pulled him out of bed. John's bed was empty. He was already up, despite the fact that he was just under five years old and didn't go to school yet.

I almost fell back in bed, but I knew I couldn't get back to sleep. It was the first day of school! While there was a good chance that in three days I would be bored out of my mind, the first day of school was kind of fun. If I missed it I wouldn't learn the rules, and I might get stuck sitting next to a girl. I didn't want to start the year off on the wrong foot.

I got dressed and headed downstairs. Mom was racing around the kitchen. "Matthew, help Christopher with his oatmeal, will you?" she asked frantically.

Christopher was one of my twin brothers. I had six brothers in all, ranging from about two years to ten. Christopher was almost two and was still learning to eat right. He had abandoned his spoon and was cramming oatmeal into his mouth—most of it was falling onto his lap.

"Christopher," I said, hoping to sound helpful, "don't forget to eat the food on your lap."

Christopher looked down, grabbed a clump of mush from his lap, and shoved it in his mouth.

John was already at the table. My other four brothers were nowhere to be seen. Three-year-old Jacob was likely still asleep. I could hear the other twin, Robin, singing back in the bathroom. John, the twins, and Jacob didn't have to go to school. But Simon and Peter were going to miss the bus if they didn't hurry.

I sat down, grabbed a bowl, ladled some oatmeal into it, and then dropped a large clump of brown sugar on the top. I glanced over to see if Mom was looking. She had her back turned, so I dropped a second clump into my bowl.

"Not too much sugar in your oatmeal," Mom said.

I quickly stirred up my mush, and it turned a pleasant brown color.

Simon wandered downstairs looking sleepy. His dark hair was sticking up at odd angles, and he was rubbing his eyes underneath his thick glasses. He had likely stayed up late last night, reading books by the light in the hall.

He sat down and put his head on the table. Simon didn't usually have the energy to eat breakfast.

"Peter!" Mom called, "you have thirty seconds to get to this table or you will miss breakfast!"

I heard a thump upstairs. Peter could be moved to do all sorts of things over the threat of missing food.

Mom put a cookie sheet covered with bread, butter, cinnamon, and sugar into the oven. There was no way our toaster could mass-produce enough slices to keep everybody happy, so Mom toasted bread in the oven.

Mom closed the oven door and then stirred a pot of hot chocolate on the stove. We didn't always get such a nice spread, but Mom tried to make the first day of school special.

"Simon, can you get me the lunch boxes?"

Too tired to argue, Simon went to the cupboard and pulled out our new lunch boxes. I had a Transformers lunch box, Simon had picked a Star Wars one, and Peter had chosen Scooby-Doo. With our new school clothes and our cool lunch boxes, I knew that the Buckleys would be looking sharp today. If only Mom had gotten the sunglasses like I asked.

Peter came into the kitchen in a shirt and underwear, pulling Jacob by the hand. He grabbed a bowl, filled it, and began to eat. Jacob climbed into a chair by John.

"Peter Buckley," Mom said, "you can't go to school in your underwear!"

"But I can't go without eating!" Peter said.

Simon looked up from the table. "So you'd rather go with a full belly than something covering up your bottom?"

I laughed and Peter shot me a mean look.

"I'm hungry," Peter said.

Mom was throwing things into the lunch boxes. She started to head up to get Peter's pants, but stopped to put Christopher back into his chair. He had tried to climb up onto the table to get more oatmeal. Dad always left at dawn for work, so Mom was pretty much left to orchestrate the entire breakfast routine by herself.

Robin toddled into the kitchen and started asking for food. Mom put him in a chair, scooped up some oatmeal for both him and Jacob, and gave them spoons.

In running mode now, Mom didn't just move from one place to another, she dashed. After getting Robin and Jacob eating, she ran out of the room to get Peter's pants.

That was about the time the smoke alarm went off.

The kitchen erupted. John, who didn't like loud noises, quickly covered his ears with his hands. He forgot he was holding a spoon full of oatmeal. A large glob of the sticky paste smacked him on the side of his face. I burst out laughing.

"Hey! Who's throwing oatmeal?" he shouted over the din, and then started crying.

Jacob, who was so startled he almost fell out of his chair, started screaming and laughing. He saw John with the oatmeal on his face and decided that there must be a food fight going on. He reached into his bowl, grabbed a wad of oatmeal, and threw it at John. Robin, who thought maybe John was making the siren noise, started smacking him with a spoon.

Peter grabbed his bowl and headed into the front room, but ran into Mom who had barreled down the stairs to try to save the toast. Peter and his oatmeal went flying. Mom didn't stop. She ran to the oven, which was now pouring out black smoke. The toast was brittle and black. Simon was laughing, and I, fearful of getting hit with flying food, took my bowl under the table to eat in peace.

Summer had ended, and school was about to begin.

CHAPTER 2

That Wasn't a Cat

I paused before getting onto the bus. I looked over my shoulder at our house. It had been a good summer. Sure, a few bad things had happened. We had gotten some chickens, and while I'd thought that would be fun at first, it ended up being a lot of work and a lot of craziness. But still, it had been kind of exciting overall.

And we had gotten into a fight with some bullies—the Hagbarts—over the Fourth of July. That hadn't been good at all, even though we "won." I was a little nervous about running into Gil Hagbart, who was my age. Hopefully the Hagbarts had forgotten the incident.

But summer was over, and I had to go back to school. I would be separated from my brothers and kind of on my own seven hours a day. I turned and slowly got on the bus, resigning myself to my fate.

Simon and Peter had gotten on before me. They were already sitting down, so I took the next empty seat and sat by myself. I looked out the window as my house slowly moved away.

I was excited about my new class and my new teacher, but I was also a little sad. Summers were freedom, and school was one big schedule. You had to be dressed and done with breakfast in time to catch the bus. Then you had to be in the building by the time the bell rang. Then you had to do math when it was math time, spelling when it was spelling time, and history when it was history time. Of course there were breaks, but it was almost like the breaks were just long enough to remind you that you were a kid and should be enjoying a beautiful fall day. Just when things were getting fun out on the soccer field, you were summoned back into the school so you could memorize the capital of Indiana. I wasn't planning on going to Indiana anytime soon. But if I did, I was pretty sure that somebody there could point me in the direction of the capital.

I couldn't see my house out of the side window, so I turned around and peered out the back. The dust from the dirt road was slowly obscuring my house from view. It was a bright day, and it looked for all the world like it was still summer. I should have been walking out our back door in shorts, giving a leftover bit of breakfast to my dog Farding, and spending the day being bored out of my mind.

Farding was a great dog. When we first got him, we thought he would turn into a big, protective, noble animal. Instead, he was short, wobbly, and didn't look that bright. But we loved him. It was Simon's idea to name him Farding since the dog had dark cheeks, and "farding" meant applying makeup. It often provided us with a good source of entertainment. Like the time the bishop of our ward had come over to visit us.

It started with, "My goodness, that's a . . . special-looking dog you have there. What's its name?"

I could tell the bishop had used the word *it* because he didn't know if Farding was a boy or a girl, so I thought I would drop the word *he* in there, to prevent confusion. I didn't want word getting out that we had a female dog in our house.

"He's Farding," I said.

"Oh, he is, is he? Does he have that problem a lot?" The bishop looked a bit flustered. "But what did you say his name was?"

Then there was the time John was giving a talk in church and told the congregation that he loved his mom, his dad, and he especially loved Farding.

My reverie was interrupted by "Turn around and sit straight! You can't sit backwards on my bus!"

I quickly turned around. Sunny was always reminding us kids of all of the bus rules. Sunny had so many rules that you couldn't hope to learn or remember them all. Your best bet was to quickly find a seat and then hide. If the bus driver couldn't see or hear you, then you usually weren't breaking any rules.

"And no talking!"

Another of Sunny's rules was that you took the first available seat after getting on the bus. The first person to get on sat on the first seat on the right-hand side. The second person to get on sat next to him or her. The third sat across, and so on and so forth. Simon and Peter, my two brothers, had gotten on before me, so they were sitting across the aisle and in front of me.

Simon sat hunched over a book, busy reading as usual. Peter was sitting next to Simon. He had smuggled a muffin onto the bus, a serious violation of the rules, and was savoring every bite. Where Simon and I had dark hair like our dad, Peter had light hair, taking after Mom. He was taller than me, a fact that every uncle and aunt seemed to have to point out whenever we went to family reunions.

Peter also had a brown paper bag on his lap. It wasn't his lunch—that was tucked away in his backpack. The bag on Peter's lap was filled with chicken feet. The last thing we'd done with the chickens was to slaughter them for meat. We'd spent last Saturday killing, plucking, and freezing our chickens. Last night Peter had gathered up a pile of chicken feet to take for show-and-tell. I wasn't sure if he'd asked Mom for permission, but I kind of doubted it.

I wanted to lean across the aisle and talk to them. Simon would probably just keep reading, and Peter would be more focused on his food, but it would be nice to at least talk to them about the first day of school. What if one of us got a mean teacher? What if some of our friends had moved away? What if third grade was too hard for me—what if they held me back?

But while quiet talking was allowed with your seat neighbor, leaning and talking across the aisle usually led to a reprimand. Whenever I peeked over the seat it seemed like Sunny was glaring at me in the big rearview mirror. I don't know how he drove the bus, because he was never looking at the road.

The bus slowed and came to a stop. I glanced out the window and noticed that we were stopping at a new house. I cringed. If there was a girl in this house, I'd have to sit by her for the whole forty minutes. It wasn't that I had anything against girls, but they made me nervous. I hunched over in my seat and heard Sunny growl from the front of the bus, "Move to the back of the bus and sit down in the first available seat."

I sat and stared at the back of the seat in front of me. It was metal with a large green cushion around the edge. Across the top was another piece of padding. It was surrounded by plastic, and for some reason I always had a strong desire to chew on it. I had never actually tried it, as I was sure Sunny would not approve of somebody chewing on his bus.

The new kid stopped by my seat. My head was down, and I stared at the floor. I could see his shoes. They looked like boy shoes, but I couldn't be sure. I didn't dare make eye contact, as that would then mean I might have to say something. Usually, when I talked to other kids I said something silly. It was better just to be quiet.

"Do I really have to sit here, or can I choose another seat?"

It was a boy. Or if not a boy, a girl with a boy's voice. I still didn't dare make eye contact. I wondered if he was asking me the question or somebody else, but before I could decide, Sunny hollered from the front of the bus.

"Sit down—we're on a tight schedule here!"

The kid sat down. There was an awkward moment of silence. I finally dared to glance over.

My suspicions were correct. The person who sat next to me was indeed a boy. He looked older than me, maybe even older than Simon. He was big, but not as big as the junior high and high school kids that got on the bus. He was thin with longish hair that almost covered his eyes. He looked relaxed, which was the opposite of what I was feeling.

I knew most of the kids at the school. I had met my teacher at a back-to-school function a few nights ago and had seen my schoolroom. I knew where to go, I knew how to get lunch, and I knew which bus to get back on—which could be particularly tricky when they all lined up at the end of the day. But I was so nervous it felt like my breakfast was doing barrel rolls down in my stomach.

But this boy, who was brand-new and couldn't possibly know everything I did, seemed calm and collected.

He glanced over at me and smiled. "Sorry, when I asked if I had to sit here, I didn't mean that I didn't want to. I just didn't want to sit down if you had a friend coming, you know."

I didn't know, but I nodded. It seemed like a safe thing to do.

He held out his hand. "I'm Allen. A-L-L-E-N, not A-L-A-N. What grade are you in?"

It seemed strange to shake another kid's hand. That seemed to be something adults did. I took his hand and shook it nervously. I was so preoccupied with wiping my hand on my pants, making sure I didn't squeeze too hard, and trying to count what seemed like an appropriate number of shakes, that I almost forgot to answer his question.

"Oh," I said, "third."

"Me too."

I was surprised. He looked older than any of the other kids I knew in third grade.

He looked over. "You might as well ask me."

I didn't know what to ask.

"You're thinking I look too old to be in third grade, right?"

I shook my head quickly. For some reason I thought that it might offend him if he knew I was thinking exactly what he told me I was thinking.

"I am old to be in third grade," he said casually. "I'm ten."

Ten! That was as old as Simon! He was two years older than me!

Allen grinned. "Go ahead and ask me."

Again, I didn't know what to ask him. Even the older kids in my grade were only nine. The only way Allen could be ten and in third grade was if he . . .

"I was held back a year," he said casually, as if telling me the color of his hair. "My birthday was two days ago, so I just turned ten. My birthday was on the border, and my parents decided to wait. And then in kindergarten they held me back a year."

Kindergarten! I had heard of kids being held back in third or fourth grade, but not in kindergarten. Kindergarten was just snacks and coloring. What could you possibly do to be held back in kindergarten? Could he not get his snack packs open? Did he eat too many crayons? You could get away with eating a little bit of glue, but not crayons.

"You might as well ask me," Allen said.

I glanced over at him again. This kid seemed to want me to ask him a lot of questions. I couldn't possibly ask him why he was held back in kindergarten.

"I colored all of my pictures using nothing but black crayons," he said, then sat back and looked toward the front of the bus. He seemed to be bored with the one-sided conversation.

Now that I finally had a question to ask, he didn't seem to want to talk. We sat in silence for a few minutes.

Allen seemed like a nice kid. Normally when I spoke to people at school, I couldn't talk the same way I could talk to my brothers. I would get nervous and say the wrong thing. And whenever I had to talk to girls, it ended up with them just giggling and me turning red. And when I talked to boys, it often ended up with me getting punched in the stomach. But Allen seemed to be talking to me just like my brothers did. He was just talking.

And now that I thought about it, he wasn't that much older than me. If he had just turned ten, and I was almost nine, then we were really only a year and a few months apart.

I glanced over at him again. He had his arms folded and looked like he'd settled in for the long bus ride.

"Why did you color everything in black?" I finally asked.

He looked over, a grin slowly spreading across his face. "Because it drove the teacher crazy. Plus, I was trying to learn how to color inside of the lines. It seemed like since all the lines were black, when I colored with black and went outside the lines, you couldn't tell as much. If I had known they were going to hold me back for it, I would have used red or something."

I didn't know what to say, but I wanted to keep talking. "Yeah, I like red. It's a good color. Especially if you're drawing war scenes."

He laughed. "Yeah, red is a good color." He thought for a minute and then said, "Hey, you should come over to my house after school. We could play Ping-Pong or something."

Ping-Pong! My uncle had a Ping-Pong table, and we would play it whenever we went over to his house. Simon always beat me, but I was getting better. "Yeah, that would be fun," I answered. "But don't you have to ask your mom or something?"

"No. Both my mom and dad work. They don't care what I do as long as I don't make a mess or burn the house down or something."

"Do you have any brothers or sisters?" I asked.

"Nope, it's just me," he replied. "It's pretty nice. I have my own bedroom and then a toy room. I have a ton of toys."

Two rooms! This kid had two rooms that were his! I shared a bedroom with four brothers. I couldn't even imagine what it would be like to have my own room. *Wow.* I wouldn't always be tripping over my brothers' junk—I would just trip on my own junk.

"Yeah, I'll come over. But I'll have to ask my mom first," I said.

"Okay, come over whenever you want."

I wondered about going over to his house without parents there. Mom might mind, but then again, she might not. I could invite a brother along, but then I'd have to share the Ping-Pong playing. And technically, Allen had just invited *me.*

There was a loud thump and a slight bump. The bus had just ran over something. For a brief second nobody did anything, but then everybody was suddenly standing or leaning to try to see what had been hit. Sunny hit the brakes and yelled, "Sit down and shut your yappers! It was just a cat."

Everyone quieted as the bus started going again. Allen remained standing and looked out the back window, ignoring Sunny's loud "Sit down!" After a moment, he came back.

"That wasn't a cat," he said, a sly look on his face.

"What was it?" I asked, but before he could answer, the air filled with an all-too-familiar stench.

"Eeww!" Kids from all over the bus started holding their noses as the smell became stronger.

"I'm warning you!" Sunny called back again. "So help me, I'll make every last one of you walk."

"Well, it looks like I won't have any problem finding the bus to go home," Allen said. "It's the skunk-bus."

We both laughed. I was going to like Allen.

When we got to school, kids jumped off the bus with shouts and giggles. Since it was the first day of school, everybody seemed to be full of nervous energy, and the skunk stench just added to the excitement. A few kids ran directly to the playground. To me, trying to play before school seemed pointless. There really wasn't time to organize and play a good game of football or soccer. Besides, today I needed time to adjust to the new surroundings.

Allen proved to be a good friend right off the bat. Once I got to class, I found out that I was supposed to be sitting right between two girls in class. And close to the front. But when we got to the classroom, Allen went up and talked to the teacher. He explained that he was new in the school, and was a bit nervous. He had made a "new friend" on the bus, and before I knew it, I found myself in the back, sitting next to Allen.

The teacher stood and welcomed the class. The room grew quiet. The first day of school was not to be taken lightly. From now on we would study, read, take tests, line up for lunch, work on projects, and listen to the teacher for seven hours a day, five days a week, four weeks a month for the next nine months. There was a lot at stake. Would we like our teacher? Would we like each other? And possibly most important, what was the bathroom policy? During summer you could go to the bathroom when you needed to. But now all bets were off. You could only use the facilities during the allotted time. Last year my teacher had very strict rules, and frowned upon those who couldn't use the bathroom during recess. There was that most unfortunate incident last year when I forgot to go during recess and then didn't dare ask the teacher. My reward was a cruel nickname for about four months.

The teacher began reciting rules. She was writing the rules on the board, so I would just read them after they were all up there. I tuned her out and looked around.

It seemed like every inch of the wall had something stapled, taped, or tacked to it. Chalkboards, presidential portraits, world maps, country maps, state maps, and mathematical figures all seemed to be competing for attention in a buzz of color and shapes.

I scowled as I noticed that at the very top of the room was taped every letter of the alphabet—in cursive. I hated cursive. At least when I wrote normally I could read what I'd written. But when I wrote in cursive, *nobody* could read it. If I already could write one way, why learn another? What was next, italics? Bold? Did you use a bigger pencil to write in bold? There were still so many things I didn't know.

I pulled out my journal, or as I called it, my *Book of Injustices,* to copy down the class rules. I'd once planned to use all the information I'd gathered to show my parents how unfair it was growing up with so many brothers. But after reading through it this summer, I found that sometimes my family could be pretty funny. However, I still used it to record an injustice whenever I found one. The nice thing about my *Book of Injustices* was that I could write in it without following any rules. There was only one sentence in cursive in the entire book, and that sentence read, "Cursive is an injustice, and it looks plain silly." At least that's what I thought it said. It was hard to read.

I looked back up to the board. The teacher was erasing the class rules.

Rats.

I looked over at Allen, who was looking out the window. Hopefully there weren't any rules outside the normal "no talking, no hitting, no spitting, and no gum." If there were any like "don't sit staring off into space while the teacher is talking," we were all going to be in a whole heap of trouble.

The quiet of the early morning was beginning to wear off as kids began whispering or asking questions. I recognized most everybody and even knew a lot of names. Some I knew from church; others I hadn't seen since last spring.

I was trying to identify all the kids by the backs of their heads when I saw Gil. My heart skipped a beat. Gil was a Hagbart and not a very nice person. He was one of the four brothers that we'd had a fight with over the summer. The Hagbarts had been picking on Simon, so Peter and I got involved. The end result was that we watched the Fourth of July fireworks from the car.

The teacher had just begun spelling when the recess bell rang. Allen hit me in the shoulder. "Come on, let's get out of here!"

We both ran out into the sunshine. It was a warm day, and we had a good sixteen minutes to run and play. We hit the swings first and then the playground equipment. A few older boys started up a game of football, and Allen asked if I wanted to come. Sometimes I liked playing football, but some of the kids were sixth graders. I found that when I played with the sixth graders, I never got the ball passed to me and was usually called "squirt."

"No, you go ahead," I answered, "I'm just going to stay here."

Allen ran to the field, and I decided to explore. I walked around the school. It looked about the same as it did last spring when we left it. I pretended I was a policeman looking for a bomb. I wouldn't defuse it because it was every kid's secret dream for their school to blow up, but I needed to find it so I could alert all of the other kids and send them to safety. I would, of course, be a hero. I stood there imagining myself receiving a medal of honor from the mayor. I was just wondering about wearing suspenders so that when they pinned the medal on me I could stick my thumbs in them, when the next thing I knew I was on the ground. Somebody had pushed me from behind. Hard.

Both hands stung where I'd hit the blacktop, and my head had just missed rebounding off the rock and tar.

"What—?" I started to say as I rolled over to see my assailant—assailants. There were three boys standing over me. Their clothes were disheveled and dirty. All three had dark hair, and in my opinion, ugly faces.

The Hagbarts had found me.

CHAPTER 3

I'm Going to Kill You

"You're not so tough without your brothers, are you Buck-Lee?" Gil sneered. He was flanked by his twin older brothers. I knew if I tried to get up I would just get pushed back down again, so I just lay there.

I looked around, my heart beating hard inside my chest, and it didn't seem like I could suck in enough air. We were near the back door of the school. If I could make it to the school, I would probably be safe. But the Hagbarts were between me and the door. There were a few other kids around, but nobody had really noticed that there was a fight going on. Although I guess with me just lying there, it wasn't exactly a fight. But even if anybody else noticed, I doubted anyone would come to my aid.

Gil stepped forward and kicked me. I was able to get my arm in front so the kick didn't land in my ribs, but it still hurt.

"We're going to get you and your brothers back for what you did to us," Gil informed me.

He kicked me again. "Ow!" I yelled, not so much in pain, but in hopes that if he thought he was hurting me, the fight would be over quicker.

Gil put one leg over me and sat down on my chest.

"Look, Buck-Lee"—Little bits of spittle flew out of his mouth and landed on my face—"I'm going to give you a knuckle-noogie until you say 'uncle.'"

I had never heard of this uncle thing before, but it didn't sound so bad.

"Uncle," I said quickly. "Uncle!"

Gil looked confused for a moment. "No—you don't—you have to wait—" Gil frowned for a moment, but then put me in a headlock, scraping his knuckles across the top of my head.

"OW!" I yelled; this time I didn't have to pretend. The top of my head burned. "Quit it!" I yelled. "I already said uncle!"

The bell rang, but that didn't stop Gil. I tried to get away, but Gil's grip was too tight. He continued to rub his knuckles across my scalp until I was sure something up there was going to catch fire. After what seemed like an eternity, Gil released me, stood up, and gave me one last kick in the ribs. Then he and his brothers walked away laughing.

I sat there for a minute, breathing hard. My arms and head hurt. I looked down at my hands—they seemed okay. But my heart sank when I saw that one of the knees on my new pants was torn. Mom had told me to be careful, and here it was the first day of school, and my pants were already ripped.

I stared after the bullies. For a moment I wished I was Superman, not so that I could beat them up, but so that I could fry them with my heat vision. I squinted my eyes at them, willing beams of molten light to shoot out and burn them to a crisp. Right then I hated those boys. I squinted so hard a few tears came out. I hurried and stood up, wiping away the tears and dirt.

It was going to be a long year.

I didn't tell Allen or the teacher about the one-sided fight. Whenever I got beat up, I felt embarrassed and weak. If I told Allen, he might think I was a sissy. And I had learned long ago that it was pointless to tell the teacher. She might discipline the bully, but she couldn't be out on the playground or in the lunch room all of the time. Sooner or later the bully would get even. It was best if I just kept the whole incident to myself. I would tell Simon after school, but nobody else.

The rest of the school day was uneventful, but only because I took precautions. I didn't go outside for lunch or the afternoon recess. When we were lining up to go to lunch, Gil walked past me and stomped on my foot, but other than that, I was able to avoid any further incident with the Hagbarts. In class, Gil sat toward the front on the side where the teacher usually sat, so all he could do during class was sneak a dirty look in my direction every once in a while.

After school I waited by the bus. Allen walked over.

"What are you doing?"

"I wanted to talk to my brother, Simon," I replied, "so we have to get on at the same time so we can sit by each other. It's the rules."

Allen glanced up at Sunny. "This bus has some crazy rules," he muttered under his breath. He started to get on, then stopped. "Are you coming over this afternoon to play Ping-Pong?"

I had forgotten about going over to play. "I'll ask my mom," I promised.

Sunny growled from inside the bus, "Get on the bus, or get off the bus, but don't just stand there. You're blocking traffic!"

Allen just stood there, staring at Sunny. Then, slowly glancing back at me and rolling his eyes, he climbed onto the bus.

Simon finally came and I followed him onto the bus. I noticed one of his sleeves was ripped a bit in the back.

We sat down in the first empty seat.

"What happened to your shirt?" I asked, already guessing the answer.

"The Hagbarts picked on me at lunch."

The feelings of hate started to bubble up again. I clenched one of my hands into a fist. Those dirty rotten Hagbarts!

"They got Peter too," Simon said. "The twins weren't involved, but Gil and a kid Peter's age picked on him this afternoon." I poked my head up over the seats and saw Peter sitting a few seats behind us. He was in first grade now, so he attended all day. He didn't look hurt, but he looked a little sad as he stared out the window.

I turned around, even angrier than before. I wanted to spit but couldn't imagine what kind of punishment Sunny would administer to a person caught spitting on the bus. Instead I hit my own leg with my fist.

"Those—" I paused, not knowing a word bad enough to describe the Hagbarts. "Those stupid kids!" I finally sputtered.

"Yeah," Simon said, "it's not that big a deal."

I was exasperated. "What?" I exclaimed. "They beat up Peter! And you. And me!"

"Well, I'd hardly call it a beating," Simon said. "They just kicked me for a while. They didn't break anything, and I wasn't bleeding."

"I was," I said, and showed him my scraped hands. My hands looked fine. The redness had gone away. I folded my arms in disgust.

"Think about it," Simon said. "We beat them up last summer. They're bullies—they have to show that they're stronger than us. The way they work is to get two or three of them, find some poor kid, and then terrorize him."

"Or her," I muttered, since the Hagbarts were known to pick on girls just as readily as boys.

Simon went on, ignoring me. "I don't think they're going to bother us again." He pulled out his book. "They picked on us today to show themselves they're still in charge and to get their revenge. Mark my words, if we stay out of their way, we won't have any more problems with them. We've stayed away from them before. We can do it again."

I looked out the window, hoping he was right. The more I thought about it, the more I could see Simon's point of view. I was still mad, but now I was a bit relieved, too. Deep down I was worried that I would have to put up with more attacks in the days to come, but if Simon was right, the whole incident was over. I had spent most of last year avoiding mean kids. I could do that again, easy. And Simon was right. The Hagbarts had their revenge; now they would just ignore us.

The ride home was long. There wasn't much to do but sit and stare out the window.

I thought about the day. I already had my spelling list to study, and a paper to fill out for history. They weren't due tomorrow, so I could truthfully tell Mom that I didn't have homework.

When the bus pulled to a stop at Allen's house, Allen walked back and said, "Remember, ask your mom." Then he got off.

A few minutes later we were at our house. Eight long hours after we had first gotten on the bus we were now back home and free.

I ran in the house, dropped my bag, and yelled for Mom.

"I'm back here!" Mom called. She was working on some project back in her room. The twins were climbing under her chair and over her legs, giggling. I'd never understood how Mom could do ordinary things with a baby in her arms or Christopher and Robin under foot or both.

"Can I go to a friend's house?" I asked.

"Has somebody invited you?" She riffled through some papers as she asked, but I knew she was paying attention.

"Yeah, a new kid—Allen."

"Oh, from around the corner? I'm glad you've made friends with him. Your dad helped move them in last week and said they looked like a nice family."

"Yeah, he's really nice," I agreed. "So can I go?"

"Why don't you take Simon along with you," Mom said. "Allen is a little older, and I think Simon would have fun too. Just be home in time for dinner and family home evening."

I almost protested, but then gave it a second thought. Right now I had a green light to go. I could just slowly back away, and in ten minutes I'd be playing at Allen's house. Or I could argue that Allen had only invited me, but that would run the risk that Mom would ask more questions. The fact that Allen's parents weren't home might come up, and then it was quite possible that neither of us would be going.

"Okay. I'll see you later," I said as I ran from the room.

I found Simon and told him about going to Allen's house. At first he didn't seem interested, but when I told him about Ping-Pong, he put his book down.

We went outside and got our bikes. Mine was a hand-me-down from Simon. It was a rusty yellow color, with a huge banana-style seat. It was not aerodynamic or sturdy, but it got me to the store, the park, the post office, or wherever else I needed to go that was more than a mile. And when you lived in a farming community, just about everything was more than a mile, except cows.

We headed north on our dirt road. The sun was bright and warmed our faces and backs. To our right was yellow wheat, swaying slightly in the breeze. The breeze was nice, and it had a nice effect on the wheat, but that same breeze brought the odors of the cows that were on the other side of the road. We rode in silence over the bumpy road, finding ourselves at the corner after a few minutes.

We got off our bikes and headed up to the front porch.

For some strange reason I started to get nervous. Allen's parents weren't at home, and I had only met him this morning. When I went to somebody's house, I knew both the kid and their parents, usually from church. But Allen's family didn't come to our church. I had learned about strangers in school. What if Allen really was just a kid that somebody used to kidnap unsuspecting children like me? Or what if Allen was a bad guy? Maybe he was really a super-villain, excited that we were walking unsuspectingly into an elaborate trap.

I knocked on the door nervously.

"He's never going to hear that knock," Simon said, reaching past me and banging on the door. The noise made me jump.

I took a deep breath. I was being silly. Allen was nice. I was just letting my imagination run away with me and was probably still feeling nervous from the incident with the Hagbarts. Allen was nothing like the Hagbarts.

I heard a sound from inside, and in another moment Allen was at the door. He opened it up and looked at us, a wide grin slowly spreading across his face. "I'm going to kill you," he said.

CHAPTER 4

Actually, I Think You Have My Paddle

Being a completely rational person, I turned and ran. I was halfway to my bike before Simon yelled, "Matthew! Where are you going?"

I realized that Simon hadn't followed me. Why wasn't he running? Had a bad guy already caught him? Was he trapped?

I looked over my shoulder and saw that Simon and Allen were standing on the porch, staring at me with confused looks on their faces. Allen had a Ping-Pong paddle in his hand.

I wasn't sure what to say. How do you say, "Allen wanted to kill me, so I thought I'd make a mad dash for my life," without sounding silly?

"Um . . ." I said. I was at a loss. It didn't look like Allen wanted to kill me, but he had still said it. Maybe I should clarify. "Um, what did you say?"

"I said I was going to kill you," he replied, holding up his paddle. "At Ping-Pong. I'm glad you brought your brother. That gives me one more victim. I'm the master at Ping-Pong."

Simon started laughing, and I felt my face turn red. Sheepishly, I made my way back to the porch and followed them inside.

Allen's house was very nice, so Simon and I took off our shoes and socks. I didn't really know the people who had lived in the house before, but it looked like Allen's parents had done a lot of work. The carpet and paint looked and smelled brand-new. The matching furniture didn't have any fraying on the armrests or blankets covering up stains or rips. Glass things sat on the end tables, and big paintings hung on the walls. At our house fragile things were either packed away or broken. The only glass at our house was in the windows, and even a few of those were cracked.

"Wow," I said, "this is nice."

"You should see my room," Allen said. We walked down the hall. There was a large room to the left and two smaller rooms to the right. The two rooms to the right were Allen's. The first was his bedroom and it was spotless. He had a huge bed that looked like a race car. He had a large dresser, and I realized that instead of being assigned two drawers like I had, he likely got to use the whole thing. I was looking in the closet at all of the clothes when I heard Simon gasp. I turned around and saw that he was looking at three large bookcases that nearly covered up one wall. They were filled with a wide assortment of books of all colors and sizes.

"Are these all yours?" Simon asked incredulously. It looked like a wall in the library at school. "Have you read them all?"

Allen smiled. "Most of them. My parents don't always let me get what I want, but they won't say no to books. I guess they think these will make me smarter."

Simon had already pulled out a few books. "You have the newest Encyclopedia Brown book! Even the library doesn't have this one yet."

"You can borrow it if you want. I've read most of the stories," Allen answered offhandedly.

"Oh, I don't want to take them if you haven't finished them," Simon protested, but from the look in his eyes, I could tell that Simon hoped Allen would insist he take them.

"Well . . ." Allen seemed embarrassed. "I've read all the stories, but if I can't figure out the mysteries, I don't read the answers. I think about them for a while."

"Me too!" Simon said. "There are still a few from the first book I haven't figured out. Like the one about the sword. What are we supposed to be, Civil War experts?"

Allen grinned. "I figured that one out. The clue is actually in the story. But the one I can't solve is . . ."

I'd wandered out of the bedroom by then. Simon and Allen seemed to be hitting it off. I glanced in the large bedroom, but it looked like that was Allen's parents' room, so I walked over to the second smaller room. I opened the door, and for a moment I thought I had died and gone to heaven.

Toys.

We had a lot of toys at our house. With seven birthdays per year, not to mention the load we got at Christmas, there was bound to be a lot. But Allen had many, many more. The entire room was dedicated to toys: toys on shelves, toys in the closet, and a small table upon which sat a railroad set. I realized my mouth was hanging slightly open.

Our toys were usually scattered throughout the house. It seemed like just when I had put away my toys, a brother would come and pull them all out again. Seven pairs of hands always seem to be dismantling any order my parents tried to create.

But Allen's toys were put away nicely in boxes. The closet was full of board games and puzzles. In the corner, Allen had a large bin filled to the brim with construction pieces. Another section of the room was dedicated to action figures. He even had some plastic terrain rolled up in a corner.

I wandered over to a set of shelves and saw some familiar toys. I, like every other red-blooded American boy, loved to buy, collect, and play with GI Joe figures. My own figures had seen action countless times in and around my house. I had four figures and one small vehicle. My brothers each had a few other characters and a minor vehicle or two. Allen, on the other hand, seemed to have everything.

Long ago I had become convinced that some toys really just sat on the shelves at the store: the huge vehicles, the ships, and the special-weapons collections. They were all too "expensive," and so they sat there, in crisp packages, never opened but always waiting. But here at Allen's house, these toys weren't in a box. They were just sitting there, out in the open, itching to be touched or played with. I reached out and gently touched a large personnel carrier.

I felt a sense of excitement well up inside of me. It was the same excitement my brothers and I felt when we pored over toy catalogs, planning all of the wonderful adventures we would have once we somehow purchased all of the toys. And now it felt like I was standing in the catalog. I could spend a week in here and never get bored!

"Pretty nice, huh?" I jumped at the sound of Allen's voice at the door. "But we can play with these later. Let's go downstairs and play Ping-Pong."

I wanted to stay. I really wanted to stay. But I didn't exactly know how to tell Allen I would rather stay up here than play Ping-Pong, so I followed him out of the room, allowing myself a backward glance just to take it all in one more time.

Downstairs we walked into a large family room, complete with a fireplace, a large television, and a Ping-Pong table set up on one end. The carpet was soft between my toes, and I could smell the familiar, cool musty smell of a basement. Allen had one paddle and began rummaging around in a box until he came up with a second paddle and a ball. He tossed the paddle to me.

Simon had followed us downstairs and was holding several of Allen's books. He settled himself into a large beanbag and began reading.

"I'm going to whomp on you," Allen said, grinning. "I practice all the time."

I didn't know quite what to say. I liked Ping-Pong but wasn't very good. We only played when we visited our uncle's, which was only a few times a year. But I still liked to play.

Allen tossed the ball to me. "You can go first," he offered.

I took the ball in my left hand. I was a little nervous playing against Allen. Since I didn't have that good of a serve, I played it safe. I dropped the ball onto the table, brought the paddle up slowly, and knocked the ball over the net in a high, slow arc.

Allen looked at the ball with an obvious hunger, his eyes never leaving it. He swung the paddle back, held it there for a brief second, then brought it down in a blinding arc. The paddle struck the ball and sent it soaring across the net. It hit the corner on my side and then bounced high, landing clear over by the brick fireplace.

"Whoa," I said, impressed, "you are good."

"Yes!" Allen half shouted, half laughed. "Yes! Did you see that! Did you see what I just did!" Allen flexed his muscles. "I'm the king of Ping-Pong!" He did a little dance.

I went to go get the ball. I felt a little bad. When I played with Simon and Peter, Simon usually beat me, and I usually beat Peter, but the games were close. My uncle would sometimes play with us, but we couldn't even score against him—he was just too good. And John liked to play, but he wasn't good at all. He couldn't even hit the ball back. The games when you didn't have a chance to win, or where you could win with your eyes closed, were just no fun. It was too bad that Allen and I weren't on the same skill level. He would probably get bored playing with me.

I returned to the table with the ball. Allen stood there, smiling. "You haven't seen anything yet," he goaded. I thought about trying a tricky serve, but usually when I tried that, I just hit the net or missed the table. I served another soft lob.

Wham!

Allen hit the ball and it went flying—not off the table, off the wall.

"Whoa, you are so lucky that didn't hit the table," Allen said, wiping his hands on his pants. "There is no way you could have returned that one."

"One to one," I said, just happy to have made a point. At least it wouldn't be a shutout. I did have a little bit of pride. I went to serve again.

Whoosh!

Allen had completely missed the ball. He looked around, confused. "What . . . ? Where . . . ?" He saw the ball at his feet. "Whoa, that had some wicked spin on it," he said. "I get it, you're playing dirty already!"

I nodded humbly, but I knew I couldn't have put a spin on the ball if my life depended on it. It was just another soft lob.

"Two to one," I said, and served again.

Wham!

"Ow! My eye! Stupid light! That would have made it!" Allen had hit the ball, but at such an angle that it had gone straight up, hit the light fixture, and then bounced back and smacked him in the face. The table would have needed to be suspended from the ceiling in order for the ball to have hit the table.

I was beginning to see a pattern.

"Three to one."

Wham!

"This ball is warped, let's use a new one."

"Four to one."

"That ball is worse! My serve."

Allen served five times in a row. He hit the net twice, the far wall once, the window once, and he almost toppled a picture on the mantelpiece over the fireplace. The ball never came close to hitting my side of the table.

"Nine to one."

I took my position and prepared to serve again.

Wham!

"Oh, of course, I'm using the wrong side of the paddle. I always use the blue side."

"Ten to one."

Wham!

"Actually, I think you have my paddle."

"Eleven to one."

Wham!

"Wait until you see my comeback!"

Allen took over the serve again at fourteen to one.

Wham! The ball careened off the south wall and bounced into the bathroom. Allen went to retrieve it. I heard the water run for just a minute. When Allen came back, he had his hand behind his back.

He served the ball and it hit his side of the table before landing in the net. There was a wet spot on the table.

"Did you just try to serve me a wet ball?" I asked. I had heard something about spitballs being illegal in baseball, but I wasn't sure about the rules in Ping-Pong.

Allen turned a little red. "No, it's just that I play better with a clean ball."

A few more serves and it was my turn again.

"Twenty to one."

"I love this game!" Allen said, grinning like a madman. "I'm the master at it."

I paused. I was confused. "You realize when I say it's twenty to one, that I'm twenty, and you're one?"

"Yeah," he said hitting the table with the side of his paddle a few times. "What's your point?"

"And you realize that the person with the highest score wins?"

"Well, duh," he said, like he was talking to a baby. "Come on, serve the ball. Or are you yellow? I'm going to score here, I can feel it."

From the sound of his voice, I knew he truly believed that. I shrugged. "Game point," I said, and served the ball.

Wham!

"Ha!" Allen said as we watched it hit the ceiling and then fall to the floor. "You are so going down in the next game. I just figured out your weakness!"

I couldn't help chuckling.

"We have to switch sides," Allen said solemnly. "I always play better when I play on that side."

Five games later, I realized I was having the time of my life. Allen had only scored six points total and posed no challenge whatsoever. John scored more points when I played against him, but he would usually pout and wander off when he was done. Yet Allen's boasting never stopped. His complete denial of reality was, for some odd reason, at once both refreshing and entertaining. Every now and then I'd look over at Simon, who had stopped reading to watch. It looked like he was trying not to laugh.

One of the times when Allen managed to hit the ball, it careened off a wall, hit the ceiling, and then bounced into a spare room. Allen kneeled down and put his eyes to the table top. He squinted for a moment and then said, as if he had just made an incredible discovery, "You know what, I think the table is warped. I'm going to have to adjust my game."

"Yeah but . . ." I began, bending down to look at the table. "The ball never hit the table, plus, the table is perfectly straight."

"Well, the ball had a weird spin from the last serve."

Allen not only ignored reality, but he refused to acknowledge the basic laws of physics. He served again.

"That almost hit your corner!"

"That almost hit Simon," I retorted, watching Simon lift up the beanbag to retrieve the ball for us.

"Yeah, but if I had put enough spin on it, there would have been no way you could have returned it."

We played eight games, and then Simon got up to play. He only played two games, and Allen only scored once.

When Allen and I played, I couldn't help but laugh at his boasting. It was so far-fetched that it was funny. But I never dared to say anything back to him. I thought it would be too rude. But when Simon and Allen played, Simon got right into the spirit of things. Perhaps because Simon had just discovered Allen's love of books, he started to bring literature into the trash-talking.

"Sheesh, I need the Hardy Boys to find your serves," Simon said while hunting for the ball behind a couch.

"Well every time you try to hit one of my serves, you look like Nancy Drew," Allen retorted. He immediately began walking around on his tiptoes, winking his eyes really fast. His voice went high as he said, "Look at me, I solve mysteries by fluttering my eyelashes and wagging my hips."

Simon doubled up with laughter. "What do you mean when I 'hit your serves'?" he said in between his laughing. "You haven't sent one I could return!"

"Well return this!" Allen said, and then promptly swung and missed the ball. Simon was laughing uncontrollably. "I'm going to start calling you Babe Ruth," he said, "because you either completely miss the ball, or you hit it out of the room!"

They were both laughing now, and I couldn't help but join in. I had never had so much fun playing a competitive sport. And it wasn't from winning; it was from watching Allen. Somewhere a clock started chiming. I counted the dongs and realized it was time to go. As we headed up the stairs, Allen turned to me, "You're lucky my wrist is so weak from writing cursive all day, or you would be crying in your milk right now."

"I don't have any milk," I pointed out.

"I would have given you some to cry in."

Allen waved good-bye to us from his front porch. We had biked halfway down the road and I could still hear him yelling, "When you come back next time, I'm going to kill you!"

CHAPTER 5

Nope, No Planes

The first time Mom called for us to wake up, something seemed to dance at the edge of my thoughts—not a happy dancing memory, rather something dark and depressing that stayed just out of my consciousness.

I pulled the covers over my head and fell back asleep. It wasn't until Mom came in the third time—and threatened to take away my dessert privileges if I wasn't dressed and eating in thirty seconds—that I stumbled out of bed and got dressed.

My brain always had a problem waking up. It couldn't seem to get control of my body, which felt three times heavier than normal. My legs didn't want to work, my fingers felt fat and numb. My head just wanted to get back on the pillow, and my eyelids wanted to close. Yet when I went to bed, none of my body parts wanted to stop moving; my eyes wouldn't stay shut, and my head wanted to be up and looking around. Sometimes I thought that I might be wired backward, being sleepy when I was supposed to be waking up, and wide awake when I was supposed to be sleepy.

Simon almost missed the bus that morning. He couldn't find his left shoe, and finally, in a state of panic, Mom made us all drop what we were doing and look for it. Peter finally found it down the heater vent in the front room. The fact that Peter found it hinted at who was in charge of cleaning the front room last night during the before-bed cleaning session.

Simon hopped out of the house, trying to put on and tie his shoe at the same time. He got on the bus after Peter and me, and ended up sitting next to Allen. They talked about books for most of the ride to school. I listened to them and was surprised. Simon was the smartest kid I knew, but Allen seemed to know a lot too. I wondered again why they had held him back in kindergarten.

We got to school and went to our classrooms. At one point I was called up to spell a word on the board. My face turned red as soon as the teacher said my name. My spelling wasn't bad, but all my talents and abilities disappeared when I had to stand up in front of the class. Thankfully, I got an easy word. The only hiccup was when I wrote the *N* backwards. The teacher corrected me and a few kids snickered. But I fixed the problem and was able to retreat to the safety of my desk in the back. It wasn't until a few minutes later, when I was sure that nobody was still thinking of my mistake, that my face returned to its natural color. I wiped sweat off my forehead with the front of my shirt. I wondered for the five-hundredth time why they didn't hand sweatbands out every morning before school. Not only would it solve the sweating problem, but we would all look really, really cool.

A few more kids were called up to spell words on the chalkboard. I spent a moment feeling sorry for them, and then opened my *Book of Injustices* to check the schedule. The bell rang at 10:37 and 44 seconds—only eight more minutes to go.

I looked up and saw that Gil was trying to spell a word. I remembered the bad feeling I'd had that morning when I woke up—and realized the source of it. Gil and his brothers had it in for me. Or did they? Simon had said that they'd gotten their revenge and probably wouldn't bother us anymore—as long as we stayed out of their way.

I hesitated when the morning recess bell rang. I watched Gil leave the room, but he paid no attention to me. He ran out the door, kicking one of the other boys in the shins on the way. It appeared that his interest had moved back to terrorizing the nearest target instead of singling me out. I waited a bit longer, and then followed everyone out.

I was careful on the playground—keeping track of Gil the whole time and making sure that I was always near the door. If he tried to attack me, I would make a beeline for the school and hopefully be safe. At one point during recess the janitor came out of the school, and I hung out by him, knowing that Gil wouldn't dare pull anything right next to an adult. But hanging out while the janitor empties wastebaskets isn't the most fun thing you'll ever do in your life, so recess ended up being a bust.

Nothing happened during the lunch break, and by afternoon recess I wasn't even thinking about the bullies anymore.

Which, as it turned out, was a mistake.

One minute I was playing four square with some friendly kids, and the next minute, Gil had crept up from behind and grabbed the ball as it bounced toward me. His younger brother walked up and stood next to him. I didn't even know his name.

I fought the urge to run. It wasn't that I was proud and didn't want to be labeled a chicken. I could handle any name-calling as long as I was healthy and in one piece. Yes sir—when the going got tough, I usually turned tail and ran.

However, I couldn't run away because technically Gil hadn't threatened me yet. If I just turned and ran the other kids might think I needed to use the bathroom really bad or something even more embarrassing. So I would wait until after Gil threatened me. Then I would be justified in running away—obviously from terror.

And besides, I was a little annoyed at Gil's timing. I was actually winning the game.

"Come on, Gil," I said, "give me the ball back." I tried to sound like Clint Eastwood, since he usually sounded threatening (but then he was always packing heat). Unfortunately, I came out sounding more like a Mouseketeer.

It was a bold move to demand something from Gil Hagbart—I didn't expect this conversation to end well. The only question was, how quickly could I run away?

"You want the ball back, Buck-Lee?" Gil asked, sneering.

I nodded, dumbly. I knew he wouldn't give it back, but I wasn't about to go chasing after it. Nothing was worse than being caught in the middle of keep-away. You ended up with nothing, except for—

SMACK!

My face felt like it was on fire. I thought Gil had started to drop the ball, and too late realized that he was drop-kicking it. The ball flew off of his foot, traveled all of five feet, and hit me smack in the face.

"My eye!" I hollered. "You poked out my eye!"

I don't know why I singled out my eye when my whole face burned, but it was the first thought that popped into my mind. Personally, I think it was a defense mechanism. If my eye really had been poked out, nobody could hold it against me if I shed some tears. If my manhood was later called into question because somebody saw me racing from the playground with tears streaming down my face, I had a good alibi—eyes water when they're hit.

But I didn't just feel like shedding a few tears. I wanted to sit down and sob. I felt mad, hurt, and helpless, all at the same time. I just wanted somebody to help me—preferably I wanted my mom, and yet I couldn't say anything like that. The last thing a guy whose eyes are watering should say is that he needs his mom. If you're going to say, "I want my mom," then you may as well say, "I want my mommy," ask for a blanket, and start sucking your thumb.

My anger finally won over. "I think my eye is falling out, you stinkpot!" I yelled, and turned and ran. I had my hands over my face, partly because my face really, really hurt, and partly so that I could cover the tears that were already running down my cheeks.

I could hear Gil's singsong behind me. "Ooh, I'm a stinkpot. Buck-Lee just hurt my feelings." Then, in a meaner voice, he yelled, "I'm going to get you every day this week, you hear?"

I made it to the bathroom, went into a stall, and sat down on the toilet. I wasn't crying. It was just that my face burned so much that my eyes were trying to cool it off with my tears. My shoulders shook, but just a little bit.

When the bell rang I wiped my face one last time and went back to class. Gil walked by my desk, leaned over, and whispered, "Crybaby Buck-Lee. Did you have a nice cry?"

After school I ran to get on the bus and found out that both Simon and Peter had been picked on. They'd roughed up Simon on the playground again, bending his glasses enough that they now sat crookedly on his face. Peter had been caught on the way back from lunch. They'd tripped him, then dragged him a few feet. He had a rug burn on one of his arms.

Peter had gotten on earlier, so I couldn't really talk to him in more detail, but Simon's seat was still open. "I think we should tell Mom and Dad," I said, sitting next to him. "They're going to find out when they see your glasses."

"Darn it. I thought I had fixed them good enough," Simon huffed, pulling off his glasses and fiddling with them again. "Telling Mom and Dad won't do any good. Even if our parents called up their parents, sooner or later it's just going to be us kids out on the playground. When that happens, we're going to get beat up. And if the Hagbarts got in trouble because we told on them, the beatings would get worse."

"Then what do we do?" I asked. "We can't just go to school every day and get beat up."

"I'm thinking about it," Simon said. "We just need a good plan."

"Why don't we just beat them up right back?" I asked. "We did it this summer, and we can do it again." Actually, I didn't want to get into another fight because I suspected that the incident last summer was just a fluke. I was willing to bet that if we got into another fight, the Hagbarts, who were bigger and meaner than us, would clean our clocks.

"Yeah, but remember we also got in trouble for getting into that fight," Simon reminded me, putting his glasses back on. "And besides, we might be able to beat them again in a fair fight, but the Hagbarts don't fight fair." He thought for a moment. "No, we have to be more subtle. And we just have to be more clever, which, judging by the twins' math scores, isn't going to be hard."

I thought about it, and of course Simon was right.

"Then what do we do?" I asked angrily. "I hate getting beat up." For a moment, I thought I was going to cry again, but I didn't want Simon to see me cry. His next words helped stop the tears.

"Give me a few days and I'll think of something," Simon answered. If anything could save us, Simon's brain could. "In the meantime," he continued, "just stay inside for recess tomorrow. Gil can't do anything to you in class. I'll tell Peter the same thing."

I stayed in for recess and lunch on Wednesday. It was boring, and I had to make up an excuse so the teacher didn't get suspicious.

"I want to study my spelling words so I can get a better grade," I said dutifully, then cringed. Now I actually had to sit at my desk and at least stare at the spelling words. I should have said I wanted to read or something.

At lunch, instead of gulping down food so that I could maximize playground time, I ate slowly, waiting until the bell rang, and returned to class.

We never got hot lunches. Each morning Mom packed our lunch boxes with sandwiches, chips, vegetables, and maybe fruit. We also had a thermos filled with milk or sometimes chocolate milk. Every once in a while, when she forgot to make powdered milk the night before, Mom would replace the milk with orange juice. There is nothing like throwing back your head, expecting chocolate milk, and then tasting the tang of citrus. I had learned not to spurt it across the table, since that usually got me cleaning duty with the janitor and dirty looks from my lunch mates.

Afternoon recess came and went, then we finished the day up with math. I liked math, and when I glanced over at Allen, I saw he was reading his math book like it was a fascinating story.

"Good stuff, eh?" I said, glad to know that I wasn't the only one who loved math.

He looked over. "Oh, man!" he whispered guiltily. "Can you see it?"

"See what?" I asked.

Allen lifted a comic book that he had hidden behind the math book.

"No, you're safe," I said, smiling.

After school I waited for Simon near the bus. "Did you think of anything?" I asked as soon as he appeared.

"No, but I will. I'm currently at the stage of getting rid of ideas that won't work. That way I can find the one that will work the best. Not only do the ideas have to work, but they have to work in such a way that we don't get caught."

I agreed—getting caught would mean extra pain.

After school Simon and I went down to play at Allen's again. We played with some of his toys, then played more Ping-Pong. Allen seemed to score a few more points, but he was still pathetically bad. The only thing quicker than his wild swing was his stream of boasts. It was easy to forget about the pains and problems of school at Allen's house.

His basement felt like a hideaway from the bad things of the world. But the rest of the week was miserable.

On Thursday I stayed in all day again. Gil pretty much ignored me, and it had taken all of two days for me to get sick of staying in for recess. Being in the same room for seven hours with only a stint in the lunchroom to break up the monotony makes the school day especially tedious. Add in cursive, spelling, an incredibly boring worksheet on adding, and a history lesson devoid of wars, and it seemed like a strikeout on every front. So far, school seemed to provide information I already knew, information I didn't want to know, or information I couldn't understand. The more I thought about it, the more I realized that I should ask Mom for another *Book of Injustices*.

Simon still had not come up with a plan by Friday. I was going crazy staying inside, but I could think of no alternative. I read during the first break, and then ate slowly again at lunch.

After lunch was science, which was always exciting, but it turned out to be a mixed bag. Instead of doing anything, the teacher just talked about an upcoming project.

"What is she saying?" I asked Allen. "I don't get it."

"We're doing an egg toss," he said. "This actually sounds kind of cool."

The teacher knew a crop duster who'd agreed to pick up our experiments at school and then drop them out of a plane. The thought of a whole mess of eggs being dropped out of a plane did seem really cool, but Allen explained that the point was to protect your egg somehow so it wouldn't break on impact.

"So we don't get to stand under the eggs?" I asked.

"Nope," Allen said. "The whole point is to protect your eggs."

How in the world do you do that?" I asked. "It's impossible!"

Allen grinned. "Not impossible, but very, very hard."

I pulled out my *Book of Injustices* and drew a few pictures of parachutes and things. How could you make an egg fall from a plane and not break? Just for fun, I drew Gil under all of the falling eggs.

The bell rang. I involuntarily jumped up for recess, but then remembered. For me, the recess bell just meant more reading.

I pulled out my book as the other kids left. Suddenly I realized the teacher was saying something to me.

My face turned red. "What?" I asked.

"I want you to go out to recess. You need some fresh air."

I thought of all the things I could say. "Oh no, I'm fine. I spend a lot of time outdoors after school." Or, "I could open a window." Or maybe even, "No thank you, I choose to stay inside."

Instead I stared at her. I suddenly realized I had no idea what her name was. How in the world had I missed that little fact? Could I even address the teacher without using her name? Had that been one of the rules that I'd missed the first day of class? Could I just call her "Mrs." or "Teacher"? "Your highness"? I remembered that in kindergarten I'd accidentally called my teacher "Mom." I still shuddered at the thought.

She was saying something else, but I was too panicked now to understand the words, so I just put my book away and walked to the back of the class. I turned around once to look at her. Could I plead my case and beg to stay inside? It was only a sixteen-minute recess after all. But the teacher was reading, and she was oblivious to the fact that she had just sentenced me to another beating on the playground.

I left, but paused just outside the door to my classroom. I had panicked, but now that I was alone I could gather my wits.

I looked down the hallway. If I turned to my right, I would exit the building and get a beating.

If I turned to my left, I would head deeper into the school, but eventually exit out the other side. Our school was set up like an assembly line. On one end you had the cafeteria and stage area. Then you had kindergarten, first grade, second grade, etc., all the way down to the sixth-grade room. It seemed appropriate; you entered the building as a kindergartner at one end and got spat out the other end ready for junior high.

I considered my options: roaming the halls or heading right out. Other classes were in session, and if a teacher saw me more than once, I'd get sent to the principal's office. And the principal had a mustache, so I knew he was not a man to be trifled with.

Hiding in the bathroom. That was actually a tempting option, but I didn't for two reasons. First was that the toilets didn't have a top lid, only a bottom lid. At home you could put both parts down to sit and read comfortably while hiding behind a locked door. At school, they didn't have the lid that closed off the toilet, so there was always the chance that you would fall in. Or worse, that there would be some plumbing incident and water would come squirting up. That would be bad enough if you were doing your business, but if you were dressed, you'd have a wet bottom, and that would be mortifying.

The second reason I didn't do it was because the bathroom had too much traffic. There were a lot of boys in the school, and if you multiplied that by how many times they went to the bathroom . . . it meant there were a lot of visits and a lot of sounds. Bottom line, I didn't want to sit in there for sixteen minutes.

There was always the library.

But the year before on the last day of school, the librarian and I had a slight . . . misunderstanding. She had challenged my honor by accusing me of checking out a sissy book, and my response had been to accidentally get the fire department involved by pulling the fire alarm. It was an honest mistake that could have happened to anybody.

I didn't want to think about it. Physical pain was better than the confrontation waiting for me in the library. I turned to the right and walked toward the light.

I paused at the door. I could hear kids laughing and playing outside. It made sense that they were happy. They didn't have the bullies' attention. Simon, Peter, and I were taking the full brunt of their wrath. In a very real way, we were the heroes of the playground. I should be getting thank-you notes, or roses, or something from all of the kids who weren't getting picked on.

I opened the doors and walked out into the sunshine. There were kids on the swings, kids playing football, kids jumping rope, and a few kids climbing on the monkey bars. I looked for Allen. For some reason, if I was going to get beat up, I didn't want him to see. If he thought I was a weakling, he probably wouldn't like me. But I didn't see him anywhere. He was probably out playing football. I couldn't help but wonder if he was as bad at football as he was Ping-Pong.

Gil was nowhere to be seen.

Simon seemed like he could always figure out the right thing to do, so I thought to myself, *What would Simon do?*

Best-case scenario was that Simon and Peter were safe in their classrooms, and the bullies were all together, hunting me. Well technically, the best-case scenario was that the Hagbarts had been arrested, and an ice-cream truck had tipped over in front of the school, but I was trying to keep things realistic.

If the Hagbarts were all together, however, I only had to keep away from that one group. If the Hagbarts had all split up, then it would be harder to hide.

But then again, if they were all together, that would be one severe beating.

The thought of a beating made me move. I didn't want to hang out in just one place in case the Hagbarts were roaming.

I quickly took stock of my boundaries. Basically, I couldn't leave the school. There was a store across the street, filled with candy and all sorts of goodies, but you weren't allowed to go in there. Or at least that's what the teachers said. The shopkeeper would sell anything to anybody, as long as you got there. Had I paid attention in history or geography, I would have understood why Simon sometimes called it Switzerland.

So I was limited to the schoolyard. Most of one side was just blacktop. There was a map of the United States in one section, some basketball standards, a tetherball pole, a few four-square courts, and a set of swing sets.

We liked to play a game on the swings called kick the crazy. You filled up the swings with kids going high and fast. Then runners would start at one end of the swing bars and try to run from that end of the swing to the other, right in the middle of the all the swingers. The point for the runner was to make it without getting kicked. The point of the swingers was to kick the runner.

I decided that I better kick into stealth mode and look for things to hide behind. The ground was pretty level, so I couldn't really hide behind a grassy knoll or anything. There were a few trees, but they were all too short and thin. There were bushes right up against the school, and for a moment I thought about just lying against the school behind the bushes. But then I thought of stickers and spiders. Or what if some kid decided to stick his head out the window and spit? Or what if he looked down and saw me? What would I say? That I was just admiring the backs of the bushes?

Decision making was taking too long, and I needed to find some cover. I looked around—still no Gil. But if they were searching around the school, they would be here any minute.

Then I spotted it—a bunch of tires, sunk into the ground. I'd never figured out exactly how to play on them. Some were just regular car tires, but others were huge tractor tires. It was a perfect cover for a skinny kid like me. I bolted over to the tires and dove behind them, pretending to be an international spy.

I lay on the grass for a moment and felt secure. I looked around. The cover wasn't bad, but it wasn't good either. I could still be seen from one end of the football field. And if I hid at the other end, someone could see me from a corner of the school.

If only I knew which corner Gil was coming from, I could adjust. It would be just my luck that Gil would come around the wrong corner.

So I looked around for another hiding spot—and there it was, the perfect place. But I had already wasted precious minutes deciding on this first hideout. Did I have time to make a run for it?

I checked the playground. No bullies. I hopped up and ran. At the very edge of the school grounds was an irrigation ditch. If it was full of water, or muddy, I'd be flat out of luck, but if it was dry . . .

Jackpot.

Drainage ditches were usually fairly weed-free, and this was dry, clear, and deep enough that I could lie down and nobody would know I was there until they were right on top of me.

I lay down and put my hands behind my back. I'd be a bit dusty, but if the bullies found me, I'd likely be dusty *and* bleeding, so just dusty was fine by me.

The view looking out from a drainage ditch is pretty dull. You can't really see anything except sky and the sides of the ditch. But the clouds looked pretty nice. They were white, fluffy, and moved really fast across the sky.

The air was cool and a slight breeze blew the scent from a nearby dairy farm, and the sun was warm and bright. I first squinted, and then closed my eyes. I probably had a few more minutes of recess, so I could afford to enjoy the warmth.

I thought of the day's events. The egg drop was going to be fun. I wondered when it was going to take place. Maybe I had missed it! Maybe it was today. I opened my eyes and peeked at the sky, checking to make sure there weren't any planes trying to drop eggs on my head. I'd make a pretty good target just lying there.

Nope, no planes.

I closed my eyes again. I wondered how I could keep an egg from breaking if it was coming out of an airplane. A parachute might work, but my experience with parachutes didn't amount to much. I had these little army men with chutes, but the ropes would get tangled and they ended up just falling fast. No, I needed something that slowed the egg down gently. Maybe if the egg was wrapped in something that gently slowed it down.

I thought if I came up with a good idea, the other kids would like me. I pictured myself standing on the playground with kids cheering all around me. Their eggs were broken. In fact, they had all landed on Gil, but my egg . . . my egg was still whole. As I hoisted my perfectly whole egg, everyone cheered again. Except for the girls, they were giggling. The girls were always giggling.

In fact, I could hear giggling now. Had I been asleep? I thought I was just thinking, but now it seemed more like dreaming. I opened my eyes.

There were two girls standing over me. They weren't in my class—they were younger. But they giggled just like the girls in my class. I didn't know what to do. I thought maybe if I smiled at them, they would go away. I smiled and then thought maybe I should show my teeth, since that's what photographers are always telling you to do.

I lay there and flashed my best toothy grin, but it just made them giggle harder.

I sat up and looked around. The kids out on the playground looked short. It was the recess for the younger kids. I had been asleep! The bell must have rung—and I had slept right through it.

I hopped up, brushing the dirt off my back and bottom the best I could as I ran toward the school.

Why did these things always happen to me?

I opened the door and walked swiftly to my room. (If you ran you would immediately get sent to the principal and his mustache.) I worried that I had been asleep for an hour or more, but I saw that I was only ten minutes late. Maybe if I opened the door very slowly, nobody would notice where I had been.

I slipped into the room, and everybody turned around. My face went red as my teacher asked me where I'd been.

How do you say—without sounding silly—that you were sleeping in an irrigation ditch during recess to avoid getting beat up?

I didn't think it was possible so I avoided the question altogether, sat down, and slunk low in my seat.

The class got settled down and Allen leaned over to me. "Where were you?" he whispered.

If I was Simon, I could have come up with a good story on the spot, but I drew a blank. I couldn't just remain silent, so I told the truth.

"I fell asleep in a ditch," I mumbled, embarrassed.

Allen stared in surprise at me for a second, then started to smile.

"Well congratulations, Matthew, you just learned the fine art of"—he laughed a little—"ditching school."

CHAPTER 6

Bullies Don't Have Armpits

I awoke to my favorite day of the week—Saturday. Saturday was a special day. It was a glorious day, a magnificent day. During the school year, it was especially grand. Sunday was nice, but with church and all, you couldn't really get down and dirty. And the weeknights were okay, but, like Sunday, you had the specter of school the next day haunting you. But Saturday was a day made especially for kids.

That Saturday, I tried to pretend that it was still summer. I slept in, watched cartoons, ate, played, and gave no thought to the morrow.

But all too soon the day came to an end. One minute I was fighting Peter over Madagascar in a game of Risk—he was just to the point where he was going to throw the board across the room—and the next thing I knew, Mom was telling us it was time for bath and bed.

The day was done and gone.

With so many sons, my mom liked to bathe several of us at once. But I refused to do that after I learned something a few months ago. I recalled my conversation with Simon.

"You still like taking baths with the little kids?"

"Yeah," I said, "it's fun to play with them. We have water fights, and—"

"Have you noticed anything about the water when you're in with them?" Simon asked.

"Not really."

"Is it warm or cold?"

"Well, it starts off warm, then gets cooler . . . but sometimes it gets warm again."

"Do you know what makes it warm?"

After Simon told me, I stopped taking baths with my brothers.

That night I slid into my bed. The sheets were clean, and my hair was still damp from my bath. The air was still, and the house was quiet and calm.

That calm lasted roughly eight seconds. Cowboys could stay on wild bulls better than my brothers and I could stay in bed. We horsed around in our room until the noise drifted downstairs and we were told to get back into bed. We then set about coming up with every possible excuse that could get us out of bed and downstairs talking to our parents—without getting into serious trouble. The trick was for it to be important enough to warrant getting out of bed and requesting an audience with them.

"My legs hurt. They feel all twingey."

"Sometimes when I close my eyes, and press my fingers against them, I see stars."

"Peter has bad gas, he might need some pink medicine."

"Did Abraham Lincoln's head ever catch on fire with his stove top hat?"

"I think there's a badger family living in our heater vent."

"Do I need to shave my mustache? Simon says it will attract the girls if it gets any longer."

Most of the time we just got hollered at and sent back to bed.

After a bit more horsing around, Mom called up the stairs. "If I hear one more peep out of you kids, you'll be sent to the porch!"

"Peep," said Simon.

"Peep," I said.

"Peep," said Peter.

It had been a tradition as of late to get one last peep in before quieting down.

"Peep," Simon said, louder.

Simon was raising the ante. I wasn't about to follow suit. Peter too remained silent.

"Peep," Simon said again, then giggled into his pillow. "Peep, peep!" He was almost yelling.

Then we heard it. Footsteps on the stairs.

Dad was suddenly in the room, moving toward Simon's bed with a firm resolve. With a quick motion, Dad lifted Simon out of bed and placed him on the floor.

"Go to the porch," Dad said, and you could tell he didn't intend to be argued with.

Simon tried anyway. "But Dad! I'm in my underwear."

Dad took Simon firmly by the hand and led him from the room. In a flash, Peter and I were across the room to the window. A few seconds later the front door opened, and Simon was deposited on the porch. Every inch of his skin must have burst out in goose bumps. He looked cold and mad.

"Will Dad let him back in?" Peter asked.

"Probably," I said, and then banged on the window. Simon looked up, and I waved and smiled. Simon made a face, and then hunkered down. Whether it was because it was cold, or because a car was coming, I couldn't tell.

A few years ago, when we lived in the city, Mom and Dad told us if we couldn't be calm at night, then we could stand on the porch until we got the wiggles out. We discovered that all we had to do was wail. A few neighbor lights would come on and the next thing we knew, Mom and Dad would haul us quickly back into the house. But now that our only neighbors were cattle, yelling only prolonged the agony. Your best bet was to stand there in silence for a while, and then look apologetic when you rang the doorbell.

One time Simon tried repeatedly ringing the doorbell, but Dad just opened the door and dumped a big glass of water on him.

A few minutes after Simon's exit tonight, however, he was let back inside, and Peter and I dove back into our beds, just in case he was escorted back by a parent.

"How was the porch?" I asked smugly.

Simon just muttered under his breath and crawled back into bed.

We were quiet for a good twenty minutes, and I was just drifting off to sleep when Simon leaned over his bunk bed again.

"I've figured it out," he said, a sly grin on his face.

He was so smug I didn't even bother to ask what he'd figured out; he was definitely going to tell me. The other evening he had told me he'd figured out how to turn off the light switch without getting out of bed. I didn't believe him, but when I came to bed, he had rigged up a pulley system so that all he had to do was pull a little string by his bed and the light went off. It was cool at first, but got old after the twentieth time.

"I'll call the mayor. I'm sure he'll want to pin a medal on you," I said, and then turned to the wall, pretending to be tired.

"You pin ribbons, not medals. Medals are hung around the neck," Simon replied in a superior tone.

I turned back to Simon. "What are you talking about?" I asked. "We get medals pinned on us all the time in Cub Scouts."

"Those are badges," Simon said, frowning. He seemed to be rethinking his little bit of trivia.

"Not the badges, dummy. The little metal things with a pin on the back. Remember? You poked Mom that one time pinning a medal on her shirt."

"That's not the point," Simon said huffily, but then he swung over the side of his bed like a monkey and landed on my bed. He smiled again. "I've figured out how to get back at the Hagbarts."

I was tempted to make him admit he was wrong about pinning a medal, but his comment about the Hagbarts got me excited. This conversation wasn't about light switches—or how smart he was—he'd figured out how to get even with the bullies!

"So how are we going to get back at them?" I asked.

He told me, and it was brilliant. We decided not to tell Peter unless we were successful.

I could hardly sit through church the next day, I was so excited for Monday to come. It was rare that I wanted to hurry and get the weekend over with, but I wanted to see if Simon's plan would actually work. The best thing about the plan was that I didn't have to do anything. Simon was taking all the risk—though, truth be told, even for him there wasn't much—which made the plan all the more brilliant.

My Primary teacher's name was Brother Winston, and he was one of the coolest people in the ward for two reasons: First, he had served in World War II, and he told us stories about it. He looked too old and frail to have ever been in a battle, but I knew that he was because once he rolled up his sleeves, and I saw an old tattoo on his arm.

The other cool thing about Brother Winston was his attitude. Brother Winston was usually a bit cranky, but he didn't talk down to you like a lot of adults did. If you asked him a question, he paused to think about an answer and wouldn't just brush you aside. You felt important when he talked to you. But he also didn't take any guff; if you were being silly, he would tell you so to your face. Many a time in our Primary class he used the phrase "You kids are flat out of your minds, do you realize that?"

We were a pretty special class because we had nine kids, seven of us boys. We were so special that for a while, before Brother Winston came, it seemed that everybody wanted to be our teacher. They took turns coming to our class, and it seemed like we had a new teacher every two weeks. I guess everybody wanted a turn to teach us. Or maybe they were auditioning teachers to see who was the best.

Then one day, in walked Brother Winston. He had an open bag of licorice in one hand. We had been bribed with candy before, and it often made some of the kids go crazy with anticipation.

As soon as all the kids saw the candy, their questions and comments started to fly.

"How many pieces does everybody get?"

"I hope it's not black licorice, because that tastes like the diarrhea medicine."

"I will need an extra piece for my brother, 'cause he cries when I get candy and he doesn't."

Ralph, who was sitting next to me, raised his hand and then lowered it, forgetting what he was going to say.

Brother Winston sat there staring at us until everybody had his or her say. Then he leaned back in his chair and said, "Listen up. I'm only going to say this once."

There was something in his voice. It wasn't threatening—in fact it was a bit raspy—but it had a commanding tone. You had to pay attention.

"We're going to have a discussion on—" He paused, looking at his manual, and then continued. "We're going to have a discussion on baptism. I'm going to lead the discussion, and you're going to participate in an orderly fashion."

Ralph raised his hand again but Brother Winston ignored it.

"If the discussion gets out of hand, I'm going to stop. I'll be bored, and so I will probably start eating this bag of licorice. If—" He paused so that we could all understand that there was a condition coming up. "If there is enough licorice at the end of the lesson for everybody to have a piece, then I will share. If there isn't, then you will get nothing. Am I understood?"

We all nodded our heads. And then everybody started talking at once.

"But what flavor is the licorice? If it's black, I don't want any anyway . . ."

"How fast can you eat licorice? Will you be eating it really quick or just sucking it?"

"How many have you got in there to begin with?"

"My dad can eat a whole watermelon. And he spits the seeds at our cat."

Brother Winston casually sat back, pulled out a plump piece of red licorice, and started to eat.

Within four seconds it was dead silent in the room. After a moment, Brother Winston put the licorice down and began the lesson.

He'd been our teacher ever since.

Today's lesson was on loving your neighbor, and I thought it was a good thing that the Hagbarts didn't live next door to us. If they were our neighbors, we'd have to love them, and that would mean we wouldn't get to carry out our plan. I smiled as I thought of Simon's plan and spent the rest of the lesson daydreaming about getting even with the Hagbarts.

Monday finally arrived. I woke up the first time Mom called. I got dressed quickly and went down for breakfast. I found it was actually fun to eat while sitting down, instead of trying to cram food in my mouth while gathering up books and socks.

On the bus I almost spilled the beans to Allen about our plan. But if I told him about our revenge, then I'd have to explain why we were getting even in the first place. Instead, he talked about how he had been practicing at Ping-Pong all weekend and was now better than ever.

School seemed to drag on. At recess I stayed in and read, and the teacher didn't seem to mind. Lunch came and went, and I watched Gil closely. Our plan should already have been put into motion, so I tried to determine if he had taken the bait. He did seem to watch the clock extra closely, but I couldn't say for sure.

Finally, the afternoon recess bell rang. Now was the moment of truth. I watched Gil leave the room. He seemed in a hurry, and didn't bother anybody on the way out. I waited a full minute, left my classroom, and then went out into the sun.

I found Simon in our predetermined spot.

"How did it go?" I asked, falling down next to Simon in the grass. We were sitting by a tree near the door just in case something went wrong.

"Perfectly," Simon said, smiling. "I ate lunch, waited until the twins were out on the playground, and then left the note on Brian's desk. Or maybe it was Brandon's. I can never tell them apart."

"Do you think they'll fall for it?"

"We'll know soon enough."

I started to think about Simon's plan. It had seemed so foolproof when he told me about it, but now, in real life, it seemed to have holes. What if they found out the note was from Simon? They would probably think I helped, and then they would really be mad at us. They'd had all summer to get over our little miscommunication, yet we were still getting some rough treatment. And now *we* were going to play a trick on *them*? If they found out, they would kill us!

Suddenly I was very nervous.

"Maybe we shouldn't do this," I said to Simon. "Can we call this off?"

"Call it off! Why would we do that?!"

"What if they find out?" I asked. "What if they know it's us? What if . . ."

"You're not scared, are you?" Simon asked, squinting at me through his glasses.

"No," I lied firmly. But I could tell Simon saw through my lie.

"Look," Simon said, "I discovered a little trick for whenever I get scared."

I looked at Simon in surprise. I didn't think Simon ever got scared. He never acted scared.

"I used to be scared of a lot of things," Simon explained, "but I found that the best way to deal with fear is flat-out denial."

"Denial?" I questioned, confused.

"Yeah," Simon said. "Denial. For example, what are you afraid of when it's dark?"

"I'm not afraid of the dark!" I protested. Actually, I *was* afraid of the dark, but Peter and John were more vocal about it, so every night Mom and Dad left the hall light on. I was just fine with that.

"Okay," Simon said, "back when you were afraid of the dark, what part of it were you afraid of? Was it just the dark, or was it something else?"

I thought about why I didn't like the darkness. It wasn't just because you couldn't see anything, it was because of the unknown.

"Well," I said, "when it's dark, you can't tell if there are snakes on the floor, spiders crawling on the blanket, or monsters under the bed. When it's light, you can see that those things aren't there."

"There you go," Simon said, pleased with my answer. "So if you're scared of snakes, or spiders, or monsters, just go into denial. Tell yourself that there are no such things as snakes, spiders, or monsters."

"But there are spiders!" I said. "I've seen them in our room. Once there was—"

"Not when the lights go out," Simon said. "They disappear. They don't exist. You deny their existence."

I thought about what he was saying. It sounded crazy, but apparently it worked for Simon.

"What scares you about the bullies?" Simon asked.

A lot of things scared me about the bullies. Most of them were closely related to pain. But for some reason, I said the first thing that popped into my head.

"When they get me in a headlock, I can smell their armpit. And it stinks."

Simon started laughing. "Well, there you go," he said. "Bullies don't have armpits."

"What?"

"Yeah, it's a fact of science," Simon said matter-of-factly. "That's why they're so mean—because they can't sweat properly, and all that sweat goes up to their brain, causing it to short-circuit. Bullies don't have armpits."

It was crazy talk, but I couldn't help but laugh.

Suddenly Simon glanced past me at the school and whispered, "Look!"

The Hagbarts had come into view. There were only three of them, Gil and the twins, but they were the three that had given us the most grief. Nolan, the Hagbart Peter's age, didn't have afternoon recess at this time.

"It looks like they're going to do it!" Simon said happily.

The three Hagbarts went to the north edge of the playground, looked back, and then hurried and crossed the street.

"I can't believe this is actually going to work!" Simon said, his voice trembling with excitement.

I was surprised at Simon's lack of faith. This was his own plan. Up until my moment of fear, I was sure it would work.

I watched the Hagbarts. They crossed the road into a field of alfalfa, just like the note Simon left them had said to do. It had read:

> I need to talk to you. I need somebody beat up, and was wondering if you would help me out. I will pay you. Meet me on the stump across the road on the north side (that is the side next to the football field). I will bring money.

He had left the note unsigned. It was my idea to clarify which way was north. I didn't know if the bullies would know for sure.

"Come on, get on the stump," Simon said under his breath. He was looking at his watch.

"How much longer?" I asked.

"Thirty seconds," came the reply.

We waited. So much could go wrong, but so far everything had gone right. Simon had dropped off the note, the bullies had taken the bait, and they were now standing conveniently on the stump.

Last week Simon had gone to the library to hide during recess. The library looked out on the north field, and Simon had noticed the sprinklers go off. The next day, Simon noted what time they went off. The following day, Simon determined that the sprinklers were on a timer because they went off, to the very second, at the same time.

Everything had gone according to plan. All that was left was . . .

"Now," Simon said.

We could hear the whish of air and water from where we sat under the tree. Sitting next to the stump was a sprinkler head that pointed right at the stump—Simon had made sure of that before school. And these weren't your wimpy lawn-sprinkler heads. These were the heavy-duty-gallons-of-water-per-minute kind of sprinkler heads.

Within seconds the Hagbarts were drenched and sputtering. Gil let out a shriek. Everybody on the playground stopped to see what was happening. When they saw Gil and the twins run dripping back to the playground, laughter erupted. Usually, you wouldn't dare laugh at the bullies, but there was safety in numbers. They couldn't beat up the entire playground at once.

"Who wrote that note?" one of the twins yelled. Nobody on the playground, with the exception of me and Simon, knew what he was talking about.

"Who wrote that note?!" they were all screaming now.

"Come on," Simon said, "we better get inside."

We ran into the school. I couldn't believe it. This was something out of a movie—a triumphant moment! We had done it! Victory was ours! We had bested the bullies! They had been bugging us for a whole week, and now we had struck back—not with brawn, but with our superior intellect.

We had gotten our victorious revenge, and it was sweet.

CHAPTER 7

Is He the One with the Donkey?

I sat on the couch, a sharpened pencil poised in my right hand and my *Book of Injustices* open on my lap. It was Monday night, which meant family night, so I would soon have a lot of items to record in my book. I had long ago realized that a house with seven boys was pretty crazy, but on family night, things became deliciously wild.

Monday night was almost sacred. There were no meetings at church or activities in the neighborhood. The church building itself was literally shut down and locked up. In fact, Monday night was so untouchable that it was considered poor form for people to drop by or even to call on the phone. Monday night was spent with your family, and nobody else.

Whether you liked it or not.

Don't get me wrong. I loved my family. And each year I realized how much more they meant to me. Even when it felt like the whole world was against me, I knew my family would love me.

But that didn't mean I had to spend all of my time with them. On a normal night, if somebody had the TV blaring in the living room, you could go to the front room. If somebody was practicing the piano in the front room, you could go to the dining room. If Mom was clearing dishes and you didn't want to get roped into a job, you could go to your bedroom. When all else failed, you could at least retreat to the fortress of solitude—the bathroom—with a good book. In other words, if the house got too crazy, and you weren't in a crazy mood yourself, you could always pull back and find peace and safety somewhere.

On family home evening night, you could do no such thing. The entire family was herded into one room and then forced to spend time together. You sang a few songs, said a few prayers, listened to a lesson (or pretended to listen to a lesson), and then usually had a little treat. But you *had* to be there. You couldn't even claim to use the bathroom for thirty minutes because the family would wait for you.

"Boys, time for family night!" my dad called from the other room. I began to write in my journal.

> 6:37: Dad calls everybody to family home evening again.

Above that line I had already written:

> 6:18: Mom tells Dad it's time for family home evening.
> 6:24: Mom reminds Dad it's time for family home evening.
> 6:25: Dad calls everybody to family home evening.

If the pattern of previous family home evenings held out, I figured we still had at least another twenty minutes before the opening prayer.

I flipped back a few pages. I had recorded a few random events here and there, but I didn't have to go far before I found the last family night entry. I read through some of the events.

> Dad told a joke that wasn't very funny. I said we should all hold up cards that rated his jokes, like they do in the Olympics. Simon said that we'd only need cards with 1-4 on them.

I flipped back a few more pages and found another family night.

> Opening song: "Testimony." We sang the first line, and then nobody knew the rest. John was sent to get hymnbooks, but after he left we switched to "A Happy

Family." By the time he came back with a stack of hymnbooks, we were done singing. He wanted to sing it anyway, but Mom said we would later. Instead, she asked him to say the opening prayer. He did, and prayed fervently that we wouldn't forget to sing the first song.

Another family night:

After the opening prayer, Dad gave us a pop quiz and asked everybody what had been said in the prayer. Nobody knew, and we got a lecture on paying attention during the prayer. It took up so much time that we skipped the lesson. Peter said the closing prayer and only said, "Please bless the cookies." That made the second pop quiz easier.

Yet another family night:

Somebody called on the phone. Dad had us all start singing a Primary song so that when he answered it, whoever called would know we were in the middle of family home evening.

I stopped flipping pages as I heard Dad yell again, "Boys! It's time for family home evening! Simon, out of the bathroom. Peter, John, you don't need that much duct tape, and besides, you never use it on brothers. Come on! Everybody in the front room!"

One by one my brothers were herded into the front room. Some wandered off while others were being rounded up, but eventually we were all in the same room. Dad came last, carrying one of the twins by the back of his pants like a suitcase.

Simon sat at the end of the couch, right next to the wall. He liked to hide books between the wall and the couch, and would read them when the lesson got boring. He normally got caught and had to fork over the book, but since he kept five or six books back there, he usually had enough to last the entire lesson.

The rest of us didn't really have our own spot. We were more or less nomadic. You sat somewhere for a few minutes, then you moved to a spot where home evening was more interesting. Throughout the course of the night you'd join kids hanging over the edge of the couch, lying on the ground, wrestling in a corner, climbing the bookcase, or dangling their feet through the banister in the adjoining hallway. When we got too crazy, we'd get a stern lecture on reverence from Dad, and we would all calm down, but eventually we would turn back into a mass of wriggling bodies, spreading and scooting out across the floor and furniture.

"Okay, one, two, three . . ." Dad counted up to nine, and assuming that those nine were actually all members of his family, he sat down to start the meeting.

"Let's see . . ." Dad looked over his back to the family home evening chart on the wall. The chart was rotated once a week, and there was a job for everybody. "Peter, you're the opening song. What would you like to sing?"

"'A Happy Family'!" Peter said, and Simon groaned. We sang this song a lot.

In Primary the song wasn't long. It goes something like this:

> *I love Mother; she loves me,*
> *We love Daddy, yes sirree;*
> *He loves us, and so you see,*
> *We are a happy family.*

You then repeat the song with "brother" and "sister" instead of "mother" and "daddy." After that, you were done.

But in our house, we substituted names. So we started with Dad and Mom, and then Simon and Matthew. Then Peter and John. Then Jacob and Christopher.

Since we had an odd number of names, Robin was always paired with our dog. We did, after all, love our dog.

I love Robin; he loves me,
We love Farding, yes sirree;
He loves us, and so you see,
We are a happy family.

Because the singing seemed to go on and on, toward the end, our enthusiasm waned. But when we got to the last verse everybody belted it out, except Mom, who shook her head, and Dad, who tried to hide his chuckling.

After everybody calmed down, Jacob said the prayer in his halting three-year-old voice, blessing the food like he always did, whether or not there was actually food to be blessed.

"Okay," Dad said. "Next on the agenda is business. Does anybody have any business?"

As soon as we heard the word *business,* hands shot into the air. Even the twins raised their hands after they saw most everybody else was doing it. We all wanted a shot at submitting a business item. Simon, the only one not holding up his hand, was slyly lifting up his book from behind the couch.

"Matthew, let's start with you," Dad said.

Darn. I hadn't really thought of anything yet. I was just raising my hand. I looked around for inspiration and, noticing the ceiling, said the first thing that came into my head.

"Did you know that peanut butter makes great glue?"

"Aha!" Mom said. "Does that explain your action figures attached to the ceiling?"

I looked away and mumbled something incoherent, and was relieved when I heard Dad say, "Who's next? Peter."

"I can get three of my toes into my mouth at the same time." He began to demonstrate, but Dad moved on.

"John?"

"I had a dream last night that Peter became crazy and tore apart the food storage room. It was scary."

"I did not!" Peter protested, as if he was going to get into trouble.

"I think you should apologize," John said.

Dad let everybody tell some news, one by one, even though most of it was nonsense and some of it was just mumbling. Then he cleared his throat.

"My business," Dad said, "is that you boys need to do a better job of aiming when you use the facilities."

"What are the facilities?" Peter asked.

"The bathroom," Simon said, looking up from his book.

Dad or Mom seemed to bring this up almost every month. For some reason it was a big deal. I remembered that one time we went with Dad to a big hardware store when he was thinking about putting in a bathroom in our unfinished basement. He was looking at toilets, and when a worker stopped by, Dad asked, almost a little desperately, "Do you sell urinals? Really big, wide ones?"

He seemed disappointed when the answer came back negative.

"Anything else?" Dad asked.

"Let's see, you might want to mention that Honor got married," Mom said.

"That's right," Dad said, "Honor was married last week."

"What?" Simon interjected. "Why didn't anybody tell me?"

"When did this happen?" I asked. I liked weddings, because there was always lots of sugar at the reception. How did I miss out on that?

"Who is Honor?" John asked.

"One of your cousins," Mom said.

My parents both came from families of eight children, which meant that we had boatloads of cousins. When we all got together, we tended to stick with the cousins that were our ages, but there were cousins both older and younger that I couldn't have picked out of a lineup.

"Wait, who is her dad?" Simon asked. "Which uncle?"

"Uncle John," Dad answered.

John gasped. "Is he the one with the donkey?"

One of my uncles lived in the suburbs, but had a donkey as a pet.

"No, that's Uncle David," Dad replied.

"I thought Uncle David lived in Idaho," Peter said, confused.

"He does, but that's the other Uncle David."

"We have two Uncle Davids?"

"Yes."

"Do we have any Aunt Davids?"

Dad didn't know how to answer that, so he looked up at the chart. "Okay, it looks like Mom has the lesson. Why don't we turn the time over to her."

"Did you know," Simon suddenly expounded, "that some stores sell candles that you light and then stick in your ear? They clean out all of your earwax by sucking it right out of your head."

"Simon," Dad said, "we're done with business."

"That's not business. It's just a cool fact."

"You should never play with matches," John said seriously. "Or Smokey the Bear will come out of the forest and maul you." He leaned closer toward Dad when he said this, just in case Smokey the Bear was hanging out in the kitchen. My parents looked at him with mouths open. John must've picked this up from Simon, who often took something that Mom and Dad had taught us, and then put his own little twist on the subject. He had quite the crazy story about how babies were born. Usually, the things John learned from Simon were scary, since Simon thought it was funny to scare John.

"I believe I had just turned the time over to Mom," Dad said again, raising his eyebrows at Simon.

John leaned back, and Mom began the lesson.

"The lesson tonight is on loving your neighbor," Mom said.

"Hey!" I interjected. "I just had this lesson yesterday in Primary. I should be exempt!" I smiled, a little bit proud that I had used such a big word.

"It's always good to hear a lesson again," Dad said. "You might catch something new the second time you hear it."

"But I heard everything," I protested, although now that I thought about it, I had spent most of the time daydreaming about getting even with the Hagbarts. Which reminded me of the success we'd had at school today, so I started daydreaming about our victory. The sprinklers, Gil's face . . .

"Then you can help me teach it," Mom said, quickly ending my happy train of thought. "Let's all settle down and listen to the lesson or we won't finish in time for dessert."

She had said "all settle down" because Simon had started reading again, Peter had found a ball behind the couch and was trying to hit the ceiling with it, John had started playing with one of the twins, and Jacob had lain down on his back and was kicking the couch with his stocking feet. Overall it seemed pretty calm.

"Okay," Mom started, "why is it important to love your neighbor?"

Nobody answered.

"Who is your neighbor?" Mom tried again.

I knew this one, and figured if I answered it, then maybe I could sit the rest of the lesson out.

"I know!" I said as I raised my hand. "Jennifer and her family are on one side, and . . . I forget who lives on the other side. What's their name?"

Simon spoke up. "Everybody is our neighbor."

"Right, Simon," Mom said. "Jennifer and her family are our next-door neighbors, but in this context, everybody is our neighbor."

I was confused.

"Well, you can't love everybody," I stated. "You can't love the bad guys."

Although my logic was simple, I thought it was sound. There were the good guys, and there were the bad guys. I was a good guy. Cops were good guys. Robbers were bad guys. The Hagbarts were bad guys. The world was a pleasant black and white.

I had always wondered how the bad guys became bad guys. Did their parents teach them to be bad like my parents taught me to be good? Did they have a family night lesson on how to be bad? Maybe they practiced robbing banks or something.

"Actually, you're supposed to love everybody, even the bad guys," Mom said, bringing me out of my thoughts.

This was crazy talk.

"But . . . you can't love bad guys," I said again, unsure of how to state my argument. The bad guys didn't deserve to be loved. Weren't you supposed to hate bad things?

Dad spoke up. "Well, Matthew, remember what the scriptures teach us: 'Love thy enemy, do good to those that curse you.' It doesn't matter if a person is nice or mean. You are supposed to love them."

My parents must have sensed that something from the lesson was sinking in, because Mom didn't continue right away. Although the chaos around me seemed to grow, I was lost in thought.

"So let me get this straight," I said. "You're supposed to love everybody, including people who are mean to you?"

Mom nodded.

"But what if they beat you up first? You don't have to love people who hit you, right?" I inquired hopefully.

"Well, the scriptures are pretty clear on that matter, too," Dad said. "If somebody hits you on the cheek, you are supposed to turn the other cheek."

"Did you know," Simon said, "that your rear end is the fourth most important part of your body when you play basketball?"

"Simon," Dad warned, "that has nothing to do with the lesson."

"Sure it does," Simon said. "You were just talking about turning the other—"

"Simon," Dad said, giving him a stern look.

Simon's interruption had given me a chance to think. "So when you say love . . ." I paused for a moment. "Well, can I beat somebody up and still love them?"

I beat up on my brothers all the time, but I still loved them.

"If you truly love somebody," Mom said, "then you won't want to beat them up."

Dad must have read my mind. "Sometimes you boys get into fights, but deep down you know that you still love each other. And within a few minutes you are playing nice again. But you should figure out ways to solve your differences other than beating on each other. There are certainly more civilized ways to settle an argument."

"ROBIN ALERT, ROBIN ALERT, BEEP-BEEP-BEEP!"

John had an annoying habit of alerting everyone whenever the twins were doing something they weren't supposed to be doing.

Robin was three shelves up on the bookcase, and just climbing on the fourth. As soon as John started yelling, Christopher bolted from the room. Both twins had learned that when John started yelling "Alert!" they often got into trouble, so their first reaction was to run away.

Mom got Robin off the bookcase, and Dad went to retrieve Christopher. Things had gotten pretty chaotic while Mom and Dad were talking to me, so for a few minutes everybody was lectured again on the importance of being reverent.

Mom continued the lesson, but I couldn't help but think about the Hagbarts. I knew that I didn't love the Hagbarts. When I fought with my brothers, I didn't really want to hurt them. We would always just hit each other in the shoulder or wrestle the other person to the ground and hold him there. We didn't actually try to do physical harm.

In fact, right after we moved to our new house, we found that our yard contained a ton of rocks. For a while, whenever one brother would get mad at another, he would pick up a rock and chuck it at the offender. Our aim was miserable, so it usually ended up with the target running away at breakneck speed. But then one day Peter hit Simon right in the head with a rock. There was blood and screaming and a big bandage. After that, no more rocks. Oh sure, we got a lecture about not throwing rocks, but we got lectures all the time about not doing all sorts of things that we continued to do. But when we realized that rocks really hurt the other person, we didn't use that method anymore, and we went back to lesser, more humane ways of inflicting pain.

But the prank we had pulled on the Hagbarts was just plain mean. I would never have done something like that to a brother. We had humiliated the Hagbarts in front of a playground full of kids. And I had loved it! Over the past week I had imagined so many different ways of hurting the Hagbarts that if I had written them out, I definitely would have gotten in trouble.

But now I was being told that I had to *love* them?

I opened my *Book of Injustices* and wrote, "Apparently you're supposed to love bullies."

That was an injustice if ever I'd heard one! It wasn't like the other commandments, where you had control. I could pay my tithing, even if I didn't want to give away my money. I could go to church, even if I didn't want to go. But how could I force myself to love somebody? It wasn't like there was a switch under my armpit or something.

I thought about asking a few more questions, but I suddenly realized that the lesson was over. If there was any further information, or better yet, an escape clause to the whole "love your neighbor" rule, I had missed it.

Simon picked the closing song, and I recorded it in my book and timed it as well. Whenever Simon got to pick the song, he chose, "Praise God, from Whom All Blessings Flow." It was the shortest song in the songbook. And when Simon led the song, it was even shorter. He ignored the pauses and I wrote "eight seconds" into my book.

After the prayer there was a general stampede into the kitchen. The smell of apple crisp had been wafting into the front room for the last part of the lesson, and our mouths were all watering.

In hindsight, it was a lose-lose situation for both my parents and us. We had to sit still through a lesson for a good thirty to forty-five minutes. By the time we were done, we were all just anxious to run around and scream. Add to that a scoop of sugar-laden dessert, and within twenty minutes we were bouncing off the walls, which, of course, was the exact moment for bedtime. So my parents lost because they had to force seven hyper kids into bed. And we lost because we were seven hyper kids being forced into bed.

The apple crisp tasted as good as it smelled. We had a bit of ice cream on top that quickly melted. I sat down at one end of the table to observe the commotion of the room. Dad was dishing up the treat, trying to fill the orders that came in.

"I want extra ice cream!"

"I don't want any ice cream!"

"I only want ice cream, but apple crisp, too."

And all the while Dad was trying to keep Robin, who had climbed up onto the bar, from simultaneously shoving one hand in the ice cream and one hand in the apple crisp.

Simon was sitting next to John.

"Show me again where the eagle is?" Simon asked.

"Right up there," John said, squinting one eye and pointing at the ceiling. "It's that shape next to the light, and it kind of looks like an eagle that's flying . . ."

Simon snatched a spoonful of John's apple crisp while he was looking at the ceiling.

Peter had been the first to get dessert and was already done. He had found the duct tape again and now sat taping toothpicks to his fingers. In another few minutes he would be chasing John through the house, making roaring sounds.

Jacob was eating his apple crisp on the floor, and there was Farding, lapping up anything Jacob happened to spill. Mom had gone off to change Christopher's diaper.

It was the calm before the storm. Things were generally quiet because we all had sweet goodness in front of us. When that ran out, the storm would rage. I could feel the wiggles building up inside of me. And I was already fighting the urge to bellow like a Viking and hit somebody with a pillow.

I opened my *Book of Injustices* and looked at the entry I had made earlier. There was always something going on in my family, and it was often pretty crazy. But it was a comfortable place to be. Like the song said, they loved me, and I loved them, except only Mom and Dad would ever actually use the sissy word *love*.

But I was dumbfounded as to how I was supposed to care one whit for the bullies.

There was a soft splat. John had realized Simon was taking his food, and had made a grab for his bowl. In the melee, a wad of soft apple goop had landed in my book, right under my last entry.

"Hey!" I yelled.

But Simon and John were done; their bowls clunked across the table as they pushed their chairs back. They were off and running.

Then Peter was suddenly by my side, licking the smear on the page in my book. In a moment there was just a stain on the page, and Peter was off, making roaring sounds and shouting, "I'm Smokey the Bear, and John has been starting forest fires! I'm going to maul you!"

John screamed.

I was itching to go run screaming too, especially when I heard Dad say it was time for pajamas.

But before closing my book, I looked down at the now drying apple mark. Even when they flipped apple slime at me, and then had the gall to eat it out of my book, I still loved my family.

Nonetheless, I circled the stain in the book and wrote "yet another injustice." Then I shut it and ran off to join my brothers.

CHAPTER 8

I Think This Carpet Is from the 1950s

I almost wish I could say that this was the end of the story. That the bullies went back to picking on *everybody* and not just my brothers and me. That we were now able to focus on the important things in life—like getting our homework done as fast as possible so we could go outside and put pennies on the railroad tracks that were behind our house.

But that didn't happen. The situation became more complicated.

However, things did calm down for a few weeks. Or rather, the situation with the bullies calmed down. The bullies were so busy trying to find out who had played the trick on them, they completely forgot about us.

But life didn't really get any better.

One morning the teacher announced, "Class, this afternoon is our first day at the library. Be thinking about what kinds of books you want to check out." It was a simple statement, yet it caused my stomach to lurch, my brow to become hot, and my hands to become cold.

The library. I couldn't go to the library. The librarian would see me!

I put my head on my desk.

The probability of learning anything else between now and the upcoming trip to the library was about zero. If my teacher brought in a live elephant, I might momentarily forget the impending doom, but as it was, there would be no more learning for Matthew Buckley this day, despite the teacher's unfounded excitement about fractions.

I had to come up with a plan to get out of going to the library. An idea popped into my head, and I couldn't see anything wrong with trying it out. I would fake being sick.

I looked around to make sure nobody was looking, then coughed.

Nobody paid attention.

I coughed again, louder. Still nothing.

I made a choking sound, followed by a gagging sound, which in turn caused me to really gag, which didn't feel very good, but when I glanced up the teacher, she was looking in my direction. Bingo!

I held my throat and tried to look weak and pathetic.

She went back to her lecturing.

Bust.

I thought about trying again, but then thought about lunch. If I was lucky, maybe I would contract food poisoning from my sack lunch. During recess I put the lunch next to the window in hopes that the sun might make the food go bad. But when lunchtime came, the food tasted fine, and I didn't get sick.

After lunch, I got desperate. I usually didn't like to address the teacher face-to-face, but I was quickly running out of options. During reading time I approached her desk. It seemed huge when you were standing in front of it, and even though the teacher was sitting down, she looked like she was towering over the whole class.

"I don't think I feel so good," I said, trying to hit that evasive tone that made me sound humble, in pain, confused, and completely honest.

The teacher looked at me for a moment, then said, "You'd better go see the nurse."

The nurse. I had never actually seen the nurse, and I had heard she gave out shots.

"Actually, I feel much better," I said haltingly. "I think the walk to the front of the class has really helped my . . . stomach."

I didn't wait for a response. I just turned and bolted back to my seat.

There was nothing left for me to do, and eventually it was time to go to the library. We lined up at the door and slowly marched down the hall.

Our teacher made us line up outside the library, where she gave us a stern lecture on what would happen to kids who misbehaved.

Finally, after casting one last warning look at the entire class, she opened the door. The kids started to go in, single file.

I followed the kids to the door, and as I craned my neck I could see the librarian sitting at her desk.

I wanted to turn around and run, but I was pretty sure my teacher could outrun me, and I would be forced back into line.

I noticed that some of the kids were going in and sitting down on beanbags. I suddenly had a wild idea. What if I just hid from the librarian the entire time? The beanbags were pretty big and I was pretty small. If I could just get over to the beanbags the librarian might not even notice I was there.

When I got to the door, I took a few quick steps and positioned two girls between me and the librarian. The girls immediately started giggling.

I bent over so that the librarian would not be able to see me. It was a bit tricky to walk, bent over at the waist in the shape of an upside-down *L*. The girls started giggling louder. I had to say something to get them to stop.

"My goodness, I think this carpet is from the 1950s," I said, hoping against all hope that I sounded like a carpet expert. My statement was rewarded with more giggling, but there was nothing to do but keep walking, using them as a human shield to hide me from the librarian. I kept up the facade by saying, "Hmmmm," and, "Oh, that's a particularly nice section," as I went along.

My face was red, but in a just a few moments I was hiding behind a beanbag. I had to curl up in the fetal position to keep from being seen. My face was so close to the floor that I could smell its musty odor.

Story time began, and I kept hidden behind the beanbag. At one point, Allen, who was sitting in a beanbag close by, looked over at me and mouthed, "What are you doing?" I didn't know exactly what to say, so I nodded slowly and smiled in what I hoped was a sly manner, as if we were sharing a joke. He looked confused, and I gave him a thumbs-up. He still looked confused, so I pointed to the carpet and gave him the okay sign.

Allen stared at me as if I was crazy, but at least he didn't giggle.

When story time was over, I had to hunch down even more, since the person sitting in the beanbag in front of me had gotten up and was no longer blocking my line of sight.

Allen wandered over.

"What are you doing?" he asked in what seemed like a thunderous voice.

"Shhhh," I hissed. "I'll explain later."

Allen stared at me for a moment and then shrugged his shoulders and walked off.

I knew I couldn't stay there for long because the librarian would undoubtedly wander around helping kids find books.

I peeked around the corner of the bag and saw that the librarian was clear across the room, helping someone locate a book. I could now move, but where to go? The largest object in the room was the librarian's desk, but I couldn't hide there. I was discovering that the library wasn't exactly the best place to play hide-and-seek.

Most of the books were in shelves built right into the walls of the library, but on one side of the room were some shelves sitting in the middle of the room. If I could just make it over to those shelves, I could hide between them and the wall.

The librarian had her back to me. There was nothing to do but make a break for it. I ran. It was only twenty feet, but it seemed like at least the length of a football field. I didn't dare stop and look back until I got to the safety of the shelves.

I looked around, but nobody was chasing me. All I had to do now was hide and wait. Ultimately we would line up and I could make my final escape.

I realized that by walking up and down the rows of books, I could position myself to pretty much look at any section of the library. If the librarian happened to walk in my direction, I could move to the end of the row and then quickly jump to the next row. I could also watch my classmates without them seeing me.

I watched my classmates for a while, and then noticed that something was wrong. Sitting at one of the tables a few feet away, with a large stack of books, was Gil. Gil usually spent reading time wandering the library, smacking people on the back of the head when nobody was looking.

But today he was poring over a large stack of books.

Or was he?

At first I assumed that he was reading them, but it only took a few moments for me to realize that he was opening each book to the very back, pulling out the library card, and then examining it closely. He'd look at the library card, then down at something on the table. I strained to see what was on the table. It looked like a scrunched-up piece of paper that he'd smoothed out.

I suddenly jumped. I had become so engrossed in watching Gil that I had forgotten the librarian! I quickly looked around, but she was at her desk and still hadn't spotted me.

As I went back to classmate watching, something else caught my eye. I was a big fan of *The Great Brain* series, and I had read all of them except for one. The library used to have a copy, but it had been stolen or lost. Last year, when the librarian and I were on speaking terms, I'd asked her about it so many times she finally agreed to get another copy. Lying on the shelf in front of me was the new book. It must have come during the summer. I grabbed it, only to remember that I wouldn't be able to check it out without having to face the librarian.

I wondered if there was some other way I could get the book. I tried to rationalize just taking it by saying that I could bring it back. After all, that's exactly what libraries do—they let you take books, as long as you bring them back. But you had to first sign your name on the card. If you didn't do that, it was the same as stealing.

The librarian had gone off to break up two kids who were settling their differences by rolling around on the floor and beating on each other. I took the opportunity to quickly head over to the front desk.

I still didn't have a plan. I couldn't check the book out myself because you had to have the date stamped by the librarian and you had to sign a card. I ducked down to the side of the desk and tried to come up with an idea.

"Children, it's almost time to head back to class," my teacher said from the back of the room. "If you want to check something out, bring it up to the desk."

The situation became a bit awkward. Now my entire class was wandering up to the desk, where I sat hiding. I was, of course, in full view of them, but I was situated so that the librarian couldn't see me when she came back to her desk.

A few kids gave me a weird look, and I waved casually, but I was pretty sure I looked quite silly.

I could hear the librarian whacking books with her rubber stamp as she checked out the books to my classmates. I finally had to admit defeat. There was no way for me to check out this book without being caught, so I would have to wait to read it until the bookmobile got it.

I raised the book up over my head and put it on the desk. There were so many kids checking out books, I knew the librarian wouldn't notice.

I sat and waited, preparing to make a mad dash for the door as soon as it was open. Even if the librarian did see me, I figured I could outrun her.

I heard a sliding noise above me and noticed my book was gone. There were a few kids still in line to check out books, but the line at the door was growing. I would have to make a dash for it.

Suddenly I heard another sliding noise. I looked up and saw *The Great Brain* book. Curiosity overcame me. I carefully reached up, grabbed it, and brought it down to where I could see it. Then without thinking, I opened the book to the back. It had been stamped! The librarian, with the mass of kids surrounding her desk, must have gotten a bit sloppy with the rubber stamp and just whacked everything within sight. I had my book!

I didn't dare sit there any longer. I ran to the door just as the class was starting to leave. Soon I was safely in the hall, relief washing over me.

It was not until later that night, as I sat under my sheet with a flashlight and read the book, that I realized I hadn't yet signed my name to the card. Did that make this book stolen property? I looked under my bed, where you could find almost anything, and quickly located a pencil. I opened the book and pulled out the card.

But it was then that I realized I wouldn't have to hide every time our class went to the library. As I looked at that card, I had a sudden insight: maybe I didn't quite understand adults as well as I thought.

Carefully I put the card back in the sleeve. At the top, next to the date stamp, in ancient librarian handwriting, was the name *Matthew Buckley.*

CHAPTER 9

I'm Pretty Sure There Is a Xylophone at the Summit

Dad had an announcement for us Friday when he got home from work. Since he worked as an engineer designing and testing rockets for the space shuttle, often, after being cooped up in an office for five days straight, he would come home and announce that we were going on some outdoor adventure.

"Boys, winter is right around the corner, and when the snow flies, I'm going to have to sit inside every day at work as well as be cooped up inside the house on the weekends. So tomorrow we're going to get up and head to Bear Lake."

We all cheered, yelled, clapped each other on the back, pushed the person who clapped just a little harder than he should have, tackled the person who hit us back after we pushed, and soon we were rolling around on the floor fighting. Dad left to tell Mom the good news.

Bear Lake wasn't too far from our house. You had to go over a mountain and through a canyon, so it took about an hour and a half. We loved Bear Lake because we could wander out a good fifty yards into the lake before the water was over our heads.

So on Friday night we were collectively sent to bed at least a hundred times. Before we went to sleep we each had our swimming trunks, blow-up toys, and various treasures we wanted to take all laid out at the foot of our beds.

Morning came. We ate, got dressed in our swimming gear, piled into the van, and began driving to Bear Lake. We were all still a bit tired, so we stayed relatively quiet until we reached the canyon.

Any sane person who drives into this particular canyon should do nothing other than stare at the beauty of their surroundings. The walls of the canyon seemed to go up forever, as if wanting to reach the sky. The road wound sharply, almost demanding that we take the drive slowly so that we could admire the scenery. There were beautiful rock formations, and every once in a while we could see a cave carved into the solid rock. It should have been breathtaking.

But we were kids, and about three hundred feet into the canyon, we were bored out of our skulls.

"Dad, how many more miles?" Peter whined.

"About forty or so, but it takes a while because we have winding roads."

"So how much longer?" I asked.

"About an hour. Just sit back and play a game or something."

A game. I turned to Simon. "Do you want to play the alphabet game?"

The alphabet game was when we all looked for letters of the alphabet, in order, on billboards, road signs, or passing trucks. If you found a letter on a sign, nobody else could use it. Most letters were pretty easy to find, but some proved to be tricky. We liked Jiffy Lubes, especially if they served Quaker State oil, although you could never get from *J* all the way through *Q* as you sped past.

I often thought that when I made a million dollars, I would buy a billboard and put all the letters of the alphabet on it, in order, so that a kid could quickly trounce his older siblings.

Simon rolled his eyes. "The alphabet game? Do you even have a brain up there, Matthew?" he questioned as he poked me in the forehead. "We're driving up a canyon. There isn't a billboard for another forty miles, and by then we'll be to Bear Lake."

Simon was picking a fight.

"Oh yeah?" I said, and luckily I had something to follow up with. "Well, we could play where you had to find an object that started with that letter."

"Oh yeah, you're right," Simon said, sarcasm dripping from his voice. "There is a great chance that we'll find a set of quintuplets standing on the side of the road. And I'm pretty sure there is a xylophone at the summit of the mountain.

Of course Simon was always going to outsmart me, so I just punched him.

"Mom! Matthew just hit me!"

As soon as he said "Mom," I turned the other way and looked out the window, trying to look bored. When he said my name, I looked over, trying to look shocked. Was he saying I had hit him? I was just staring out the window! Mom glanced back but decided not to get involved.

"Stinker," Simon muttered under his breath.

"Why don't you kids play the license-plate game?" Dad suggested from the front.

"Yeah!" I shouted. Anything to pass the time.

"I get eight," Simon said.

"Four," I shouted. Four was my lucky number, since I was born on October fourth.

"I get three," Peter shouted.

"I'll have . . ." John slowly thought. "I think . . . Hmmmmm . . ."

Four minutes later, John finally picked two.

Simon dug around in the back of the van until he found a piece of paper and a pen to keep track of the numbers. In the license-plate game, everybody picked a number, and then each time a car passed, you read the numbers. If your number was on the plate, you got a point. Whoever had the most points won and then argued for the rest of the day that it was a game of skill, with everybody else muttering that it was nothing but luck.

We usually played the game on the freeway and only counted the cars that passed us going the same way. It was easy to read the numbers on their plates. But the canyon was just a two-lane road.

"We'll have to count the plates on the cars going the other way," Simon said.

"We can't read all the numbers that way," I pointed out. "They go by too fast."

"Dad's going so slow we'll be able to read them just fine," Simon countered.

We were all on different benches, so we shifted to the left-hand side of the van. In just a few moments a car passed us. Simon was right, it was a bit tricky, but you could usually make out a few numbers.

"That one had a four," I said. "Give me a point."

Simon made a mark. "It also had an eight."

"I didn't see an eight," I said.

"It was going too fast. You missed it."

I was pretty sure Simon was cheating.

Another car passed, with no fours, but two threes.

"That had a three!" Peter said. "Two threes!"

"I can't read them that fast," John whined. "Dad, slow down."

"It didn't have any threes, Peter," Simon said. "They were eights. They just looked like threes."

"No they weren't," Peter said, "they were threes."

"I saw threes," I said.

"Eights," Simon said. "But I'll give you a point since you got all excited for nothing."

Peter glared back and was about to argue further when another car came. It was a vanity plate and only had letters.

"Stupid words," Peter muttered.

"I still can't read them," John whined again. "Dad, slow down."

Two more cars came, and I scored another point.

"That one had a three," Peter said.

"No, that was another eight. You just can't see them right because they're moving so fast," Simon explained.

In a flash Peter was over two seats and had Simon in a headlock.

"That was a three! I can read them just fine! You're just a big cheaterhead!"

"Peter, get back to your seat!" Mom called from the front.

Peter was a big kid, but Simon had more experience. With a twist, Peter found himself on the floor of the van, down by the spare tire.

It was silent for a moment. Then suddenly, like the creature from the black lagoon, Peter rose up over the back of the seat. At first I could only see the top of his head. But as he rose higher I could see he had an evil grin and a wild look in his blue eyes.

He held a tire iron in his right hand.

"ARGHHH!" Simon screamed, and as fast as Peter had come to the back of the van to argue about the score, Simon now flew to the front. I joined Simon in beating a hasty retreat, just in case Peter decided that he should go after whoever was in the vicinity. I seriously doubted Peter would use the tire iron, but you never could tell.

"Peter Buckley!" Mom yelled. "Put down that tire iron right this instant, or I'll tell Dad to turn this van around and go home!"

Peter dropped the tire iron with a clang. The license plate game was officially over, and we returned to our seats.

Dad suggested we keep an eye out for grizzly bears. John and Jacob dutifully pressed their noses against the van windows and kept a watchful eye out for the creatures.

If I had been a few years younger, I would have kept a face to the window for the rest of the trip, too, hoping against hope to see a bear. Whenever we went somewhere, Dad would say, "I think there are cougars in these parts," or, "They spotted an elephant around here somewhere just last week." Whether it was a trip to Bear Lake, Promontory Point, or the supermarket, when things got a bit crazy, Dad would tell us about all kinds of animals that were lurking just off to the side of the road.

But all I ever saw was a squirrel, or maybe a squished skunk. Once or twice Dad would claim to have spotted a deer, but even when he slowed down and pointed, I rarely saw them.

Eventually, after much driving, whining, and heated conversation, we hit a high spot in the road, and the lake was suddenly in view.

"I see Bear Lake!" John hollered from the front.

It was always a beautiful sight. The lake was a deep, patchy blue, encircled by dusty brown mountains. It was still another fifteen minutes to the lake, but now our goal was in sight, so the ride wasn't quite so painful. We switchbacked down the mountain and were finally driving alongside the lake. Another five minutes and the van was parked in the picnic parking lot. We all tore off in the general direction of the lake, leaving our parents to unload the van.

I should mention that Bear Lake is as cold as it is beautiful. There are approximately six days a year when the water is almost warm enough to go swimming, but we were long past those six days. It was now almost October, and the water was freezing. If I ever saw an iceberg with penguins playing around on top, I wouldn't have given it a second thought.

But when you're just a kid, you don't pay attention to details. Pretty soon we were all waist deep in the chilly water, our teeth chattering and our bodies covered with goose bumps, but yelling, splashing, and having the time of our lives.

John stood near the edge of the water and began to dig in the sand. He wore a floating device around his waist, as well as bright orange floaties on his arms, despite the fact that he likely wouldn't get in the water. Simon had told him about the Bear Lake Monster several years ago. He hadn't done much swimming after that.

The problem with going to Bear Lake was that the drive seemed so long and the day seemed so short. We played in the water, played on the beach, played in the water some more, ran down the beach, ate a quick lunch, threw the Frisbee, ate more lunch, and then collapsed on the beach late in the afternoon when our energy was spent.

"Do you realize we could do this every day if we didn't have school and Dad didn't have work?" Simon asked me.

I closed my eyes and imagined what it would be like. We hadn't been in the water recently, so neither of us had chattering teeth, and our lips were now pink instead of slightly blue. The sun was warm if you lay there long enough to soak it in. My mind wandered to school, and for some reason I thought of the Hagbarts. It had been almost a week now since we'd gotten them back, and since then the situation had returned to normal. In fact, I don't think I'd given them much thought since Monday night. I was pleased that I wouldn't have to worry about loving my neighbor.

If the Hagbarts left us alone, then, while I might not love them, I could at least be indifferent to them. It was only when they picked on me and my brothers that I hated them.

I was almost asleep when I realized it would be silly to take a nap at the beach with all these fun things to do. I got up and walked down to the beach front. John had built quite the complex of castles and moats, but I wandered farther. I found a stick and spent a few minutes whacking the tops off weeds.

Suddenly I was through the weeds and saw an impossible stretch of perfectly flat sand. You could tell by its color that it was damp. There were no weeds or rocks or anything to mar the surface.

"That looks like a giant piece of paper," I said out loud.

I'd never been much of an artist, but when you have sand like that and a stick in your hand, there isn't much you can do except draw. I tried doodling a few small pictures, but found that the bigger the picture, the better it looked.

I made a lopsided half circle with my hand and realized the shape kind of looked like a nose. I put a circle at the top and dotted the middle of it. I walked down to where the bottom of the nose was and drew a huge lip with a single buck tooth extending at an odd angle. I topped it off with an exaggerated nostril and wild hair. I stepped back to view my creation.

It was an ugly, ugly piece of art. I laughed.

Simon wandered over. "What are you—" He stopped, and I was filled with immense pleasure as he chuckled.

Simon got down on his hands and knees and began to widen the groove that my stick had made. I was almost ready to protest, but then realized that by making the groove more pronounced and smoothing out the sand around it, the picture looked much better. I bent over and started on the other end of my wild face. Soon, Peter and even John came over and started in on the project.

By the time we were done we had a really cool cartoon, carved into the sand of Bear Lake.

"We should give him a name," Simon said. "How about Wilbur?"

"How about Eustace?" Peter chimed in.

"Too fancy," I replied. "Let's just call him Bob."

We bent over and carved the huge letters into the sand.

We stepped back to admire our handiwork.

"I don't believe it," Simon said.

"I know," I said, enthusiastically, "and it's far enough from the beach that the water won't mess it up."

"No, not that," Simon said, shock in his voice. "Over there."

I looked over at Simon and saw him pointing farther down the beach.

All I could see were a boat, a few dogs, some people . . . and some kids. Kids coming our way.

"Maybe they want to play," I said, although as I looked I saw something familiar in the way they walked. And in their size.

And then I knew them, and my heart sank. We were sixty miles from home, on the edge of a lake in the middle of nowhere, and there, just down the beach, were the four Hagbart boys.

And they were headed straight for us.

CHAPTER 10

I Would Beat the Stuffing Out of Us

"What do we do?" I whispered frantically.

We couldn't run away. We had spent too much effort on our little art project to just turn tail and run. I envisioned bully's feet tromping through our fragile image.

"Let's see what they want," Simon answered.

The bullies had spotted us and were now coming faster. I thought for a moment that we could take them. We had done it once before just a few months ago. Surely we could do it now. Plus, we were all in our swimming trunks. Weren't people stronger in their swimming trunks?

The Hagbarts were close enough that I could see their annoying sneers, and I could feel my anger start to rise. Those Hagbarts drove me crazy! Why did they have to follow us up to Bear Lake and ruin our day?

"Well, if it isn't the Buckley Babies." Gil smirked. Then he saw our drawing. "Hey, what's that?"

Simon ignored the question. "What are you guys doing here? This is our beach!"

One of the twins looked at the face we had drawn. "Which one of you is Bob? It looks to me like this is Bob's beach, not yours."

Nobody really knew what else to say. We stood there for a moment, staring at each other. I felt tense. If they tried to beat me up, I wouldn't take it. They weren't just insulting me and my brothers now—they were insulting Bob! My blood was boiling, and I was ready to fight.

"We're going to get you guys so bad," Gil said suddenly.

"What do you mean?" Simon asked.

"We're going to get you back for what you did to us."

"What we did to you? You guys are the ones who've been—"

"We're going to get you back for the sprinkler trick," Gil said. "You're going to be sorry you ever messed with the Hagbarts."

My anger was replaced with a particularly concentrated dose of terror. They knew! They had figured out who'd played the trick on them. We were dead!

"Come on," Brian said. "We'll get these guys later."

There was a little bit of pushing as the Hagbarts made their way through us, and Brandon kicked a bit of sand onto our art, but John dropped down and immediately started to clean it off.

It was over. The bullies had left without beating on us. For a moment I felt relief.

"Something is seriously wrong," Simon said, his voice sounding a bit funny.

"What do you mean?" I asked. "It looks like they're leaving." I wanted to feel relief, but I knew Simon was right. The situation was bad. Very bad.

"Think about it," Simon said. "The bullies know we were the ones that pulled the trick on them."

"Actually," I reminded him, "it was mainly your idea. You wrote the note and delivered it."

Simon ignored me. "If you were the bullies and had found out we were the ones who had pulled the trick on them, what would you do?"

"I would be very nice to us, and never pick on us anymore."

Simon rolled his eyes. "If you were the bullies, what would you do?"

I didn't have to think about it. I knew the answer; I just didn't like it. Peter answered Simon's question matter-of-factly: "If I was a bully, I would beat the stuffing out of us."

"Exactly," Simon said. "So why didn't they? Mom and Dad are all the way over by the picnic benches. They had a clear shot at us. They said they were going to get even, so why are they waiting?"

Peter shrugged and stuck a toe up Bob's nostril.

"Maybe they want to do it in front of the school," I suggested.

"There are a lot of good reasons why they might want to wait on beating us up in front of the school, but the Hagbarts couldn't think of any of them. They should have beat us up, right here, right now," Simon said, pushing his glasses up.

"It sounds like you want to get beat up," I replied, getting down to smooth out some of the Hagbarts' footprints. "If they want to put off the beating, that's fine with me."

"It just makes me nervous," Simon said. "It doesn't make any sense."

A shudder went through me. If Simon was nervous, then I should be downright terrified.

We finished cleaning up Bob and signed our work. I sighed as I realized that the Hagbarts would probably have a field day stomping it into oblivion. With a heavy heart, I headed back to our campsite. As I walked, I noticed Mom talking to an unfamiliar gray-haired lady at another campsite. I wondered why Mom was talking to her. Simon's voice jumped me out of my musings.

"How did they figure out it was us? You didn't tell anybody, did you?"

"Of course not!" I was shocked that he would even question my loyalty.

"Even Allen?" Simon asked.

"Even Allen," I said. I hadn't told Allen about the bullies at all. I was afraid that if he found out I was afraid of the Hagbarts, he wouldn't ask me over to his house to play Ping-Pong anymore.

We hadn't even told Peter before it happened, so nobody else knew that we'd done it. How could they have figured it out?

"Maybe they just guessed," I said.

"No, they knew. But how did they figure it out? There is no way . . ."

I pondered how they could have solved the mystery, but I couldn't figure it out either.

Peter was picking through bags and then pulled out a shoe box. "Hey, do you guys want to play Buckley Uno?" he asked.

I didn't really, but maybe it would take my mind off the troubles at hand. I nodded.

Peter brought over the shoe box and pulled out the contents. There were several sheets of paper that outlined all the additional rules and regulations we had added to the normal game. He also pulled out the cards and began to stack them up; the stack was about seven inches tall, because in Buckley Uno, you had to use at least six decks.

Something about the rules caught my attention. The paper with the rules was creased and faded because the rules were often fought over, examined, and added to every time we played the game. But there was something else. The paper was a bit crinkly because I think we had spilled some drink on the pages at one point, and the paper had stiffened when it dried.

Stiff, crinkly paper. And as simple as that, I had solved the problem. I was too stunned to bask in my mental prowess. "I know how they figured it out."

"What?" Simon turned to me as he helped Peter shuffle the cards. "Figured what out?"

"I know how the Hagbarts figured out who played the trick on them."

"How?"

I quickly explained to Simon. The dried-out rules reminded me of the paper Gil had been poring over in the library. The paper he was looking at had gotten wet at some point. It was the note that Simon had written! And he was looking through books trying to match the handwriting on the note with the names on library check-out cards.

Simon sat still, thinking. "You're right. Why else would Gil be looking at books?" He thought for a moment longer. "But how in the world would the Hagbarts think to do that? That's something I would do . . ."

I ignored Simon's allusion to his own brilliance.

Peter had dealt out the cards, and we played Buckley Uno for a while, but our hearts weren't in it. After four hands, we all quit.

Usually, Buckley Uno wasn't over until at least two of us were rolling on the floor, fighting over a few cards. But today, we just weren't in the mood.

Mom came back to camp and started clearing things up for dinner. Peter had wandered off to look for bugs, and just Simon and I sat at the table, both of us lost in thought.

Mom spoke. "Guess what boys? I ran into a very nice lady a few camps over. She lives in Lakeview City and her grandchildren are up visiting for the weekend—the Hagbarts. Don't they go to your school?"

That explained why they were here. We both mumbled that yes, the Hagbarts went to our school.

"You should keep an eye out for them," Mom said, looking down to the beach. "They're around here somewhere."

Simon and I exchanged a glance. There was no need to tell Mom that we had already seen them. And that we were in fact keeping an eye out for them. A wary eye. And neither of us felt like telling her the Hagbarts were the kids we had fought with last summer.

"Maybe you kids should invite them over to the house sometime," Mom suggested. "They probably need some good friends."

That was enough to get a reply out of Simon. "Maybe if they didn't beat up everything that moves, they would *have* some good friends."

Mom turned to Simon, and I was surprised to see fire in her eyes.

"Simon Buckley, don't you forget how lucky you are! If you see those boys today, or at school, I want you to be nice to them, do you hear me? It doesn't matter what they do to you. You are always to be nice to them, do you understand?"

What could you say to that? Simon mumbled, "Okay, Mom," and Mom turned back to dinner.

On the way home, with my head leaning against the window, and the trees and rocks flying by in the twilight, I realized it had not been a very good day. The bully problem had not gone away. In fact, come Monday, the bullies would be focused on us now more than ever. We had humiliated them in front of the school, and they would get their revenge.

But more depressing was that Mom wanted us to be nice to the bullies. Dad wanted it too. He had even used the phrase "turn the other cheek." How could I turn my cheek to the Hagbarts? I was afraid of them. I wanted nothing to do with them. If I found that they were moving and that I would never see them again in my entire life, I would throw a party.

I took out my *Book of Injustices* and wrote, "Love the Hagbarts = Impossible."

CHAPTER 11

Not Accidents on the Playground

For one solid week, nothing happened with the bullies. And while that may seem like a short period of time, for an eight-year-old kid, a week lasts practically forever.

At the beginning of the week, I was on edge. I flinched every single time Gil moved. When he got up to use the bathroom, I went into panic mode. When he walked past me in the lunchroom, I waited for lasagna to be poured on my head.

But as the week went on, nothing happened. There were no beatings, no tricks, and by the end of the week, I had completely forgotten the incident at Bear Lake. The bullies weren't going to hurt me. They had forgotten all about it, and I was safe forever!

Several times that week Simon and I went over to play with Allen. I really wanted to play with Allen's wide assortment of toys, but Allen just wanted to play Ping-Pong. Simon explained that Allen didn't want to play with his toys because he could do that anytime. But Ping-Pong was something he could only do when somebody came over.

Allen still trash-talked all the time, and it was fun to join in, but I noticed he now scored six or seven times before getting beat. He surprised me by slowly getting better.

Simon also surprised me by asking me one morning what I wanted for my birthday.

"My birthday?" I asked. Every year my birthday sneaked up on me. My birthday was on October fourth, so when September rolled around, I knew I still had a month to wait. Since I couldn't remember how many days were in September, I just didn't pay attention until it was October—and then my birthday was just a few days away.

"What day is it?" I asked Simon.

"September thirtieth."

"And how many days does September have?" I asked, getting excited.

"Thirty," came the reply.

That meant my birthday was in four days! Today was Wednesday, so that meant my birthday fell on a Sunday. In fact, that meant that general conference was on my birthday, a fact that was even better! The only two Sundays we didn't go to church were the first Sundays in April and October, when conference talks were broadcast right into our homes. I had never attended church on my birthday, so it was kind of like a vacation.

Simon and I talked about all the cool toys I should ask for. The bullies were completely pushed out of my mind as I prepared for and thought about my upcoming birthday.

At some point in our childhood, Mom realized that with seven kids and six birthdays, she would be planning, running, and cleaning up a big birthday party every other month. After one of Peter's birthdays, while scrubbing frosting off the walls, Mom declared that we could only have a birthday party with friends every other year. Last year I'd had a wild party with my friends that had morphed into a water fight, so I knew that this year only my family would be around. But with my raucous brothers, we would still have a party.

Saturday came and went in a blur, as most of them usually did.

Sunday finally arrived, and we went from daylight savings time back to normal time. Instead of having to wake up early in time for church, we slept. Instead of putting on uncomfortable church clothes, we just stayed in our pajamas. And instead of being hauled off to church for three hours, we simply walked into the living room and comfortably lounged in front of the TV to watch the morning session. It was a great start to my birthday.

As I plopped down on the couch to listen to conference, I found John already in front of the TV. He was staring very seriously at the speaker.

"Be slow to anger, and quick to forgive," the speaker was saying.

John piped up. "Peter gets angry all the time. He likes to kick people in the shins."

"We should love our fellow men, and even be kind to those who might wish us ill."

"Matthew is not kind to his neighbor. He got in a fight last summer," John said.

"Yeah, but so did he!" I said, pointing at John, and then realized I was tattling on my brother to a TV screen. I smacked my forehead and settled back on the couch.

But the speaker's words were troubling. It seemed like ever since the whole Hagbart mess came up, all I got from every adult was a lecture on why I should love everybody.

After conference we had our traditional big meal between the two sessions. The afternoon session was our favorite because two years earlier my parents had instituted a very enjoyable tradition. We didn't have to watch the afternoon session, but for anybody who did watch, they could have all the ice cream they wanted.

While we very likely heard talks against the evils of gluttony and about the virtues of self-control, we piled up bowl after bowl of ice cream, sprinkling it with crumbled cookies, marshmallow topping, caramel, and chocolate sauce. By the end of the session we were twitching with the sugar rush and spent the rest of the day running out in the cool autumn evening.

That night we celebrated my birthday with cake and whatever ice cream was left over. I opened my presents, and my brothers and I played with toys for the rest of the night. By the time I had been tucked into my bed, well past my bedtime, I felt great, like somebody had invented a happy grenade and set it off in my room. I'm sure I slept through the night with a wide grin on my face.

With the time change, school wasn't quite so bad. It wasn't as hard to wake up, and it was easier to go to sleep after Mom and Dad's fifth yell (instead of the twentieth).

Schoolwork wasn't so bad either. I had figured out that I had to take spelling words home and look at them before taking the test. I also figured out which subjects I could afford to daydream during, because I already knew the material, and which subjects I needed to pay special attention to.

The entire week after my birthday went by in this blissful state. The routine wasn't as fun as in summer, but for school it wasn't half bad. I had fallen into a state of good routine, which is why on the Tuesday of the second week of October, I shouldn't have been surprised to find a note in my desk that brought everything back into a state of stomach-cramping anxiety. The note read as follows:

Dear Parent,

Your child has been identified as one who is prone to accidents. Not accidents on the playground; rather, accidents in his pants. We know this is a touchy subject, but for hygienic reasons, we request that you send an extra pair of underpants to school with your child. This way, if there are any problems, we will have an extra pair of underpants on hand. Please have your child bring his underpants to school and store them in his desk. The teacher will periodically check to make sure the underpants are there. If they are not there, the teacher will have to remind the student to bring them.

Thank you for your cooperation.
Principle Gary

I was mortified beyond words, and I'm sure my mouth hung open. Only instinct made me wad up the paper and shove it in my backpack before anybody else saw it.

How many kids got these letters? Was I the only one prone to accidents? My face was burning even though I knew nobody had seen the letter. "Prone to accidents?" I had never had an accident! Well, at least not in this class. And last year . . . well, there had certainly been extenuating circumstances, hadn't there? But now I was in complete control. I had just turned nine! There was no way I was going to bring a pair of underpants to school.

And yet at the same time, I knew that by tomorrow I would, in fact, have a pair of underpants dutifully tucked away in my desk. I couldn't fight it. I wasn't about to show my parents the note and ask them to look into the matter. After all, the letter said, "prone to accidents." I didn't want anybody seeing that phrase in a letter addressed to me. That was the way rumors were started. And once people thought you were prone to accidents, you might as well be prone to accidents, because you would never live it down.

And I couldn't just ignore the letter. It said the teacher would be checking. I would die of embarrassment if my teacher had to pull me aside and ask the whereabouts of my backup underclothing.

That night I lay awake. When I knew for sure that everybody was asleep, I crept out of bed and opened my drawer. For Christmas last year, all of my brothers had gotten underwear from a distant aunt. It was cartoon underwear, and Simon and I didn't really like to wear it. I had conveniently lost several pairs, but my Yosemite Sam underpants were still hanging around at the back of my drawer. I wadded them up and tucked them into the very bottom of my schoolbag.

The next day I stayed in at the beginning of recess. All of the students had left, and only my teacher remained. She glanced over at me, and I quickly looked around the class in fascination, as if I had just unearthed an ancient tomb. My teacher chose to ignore me and began reading a book.

I brought my backpack up into my lap and stared at my teacher. She seemed engrossed in her book, but how could I be sure? I slowly started to unzip my backpack. The teacher glanced up, and I dropped my hands to my side. She stared at me for a moment, then went back to her reading.

I continued to unzip my backpack, never taking my eyes off her. She seemed to be reading, and yet she seemed to be watching me out of the corner of her eye, too. What to do?

I closed my eyes, and then had an idea. I gave a big yawn, and laid my head down on my desk. I could still see the teacher through squinted eyes. She was looking at me again, but soon she went back to her reading.

I started to snore.

It was a good snore too. There was no way she could have thought I was still awake. My hand slowly went to my pack. I finished unzipping my bag and fished out my underwear. Slowly, ever so slowly, I brought my hand up, and then shoved it deep into the back corner of my desk. I placed books, paper, pencils, and anything else I could find in front of the fabric, and then sat up and stretched, as if I had just taken a nice nap.

I left the room, convinced that I had pulled it off. Nobody in the world knew what I had done. I had retrieved my underpants without my parents knowing. I had brought them to school without my brothers or classmates knowing. And I had hidden them in my desk without my teacher seeing because I was so good at faking sleep. There was no way that anybody on the face of the planet could possibly know what was tucked into my desk.

The next day my underpants were gone.

CHAPTER 12

Wait, Can You Read Yet?

"What are you going to do for the egg drop?"

School had become a source of anxiety again. With the disappearance of my underpants, everything seemed to have an air of gloom and doom.

I had the same problem as when I first got the note. Who was I supposed to tell about my missing underwear? To do that, I'd have to explain why I had brought them to school in the first place. I had rehearsed it in my mind, but there was just no sophisticated way to say, "I seem to have misplaced my Yosemite Sam underpants. Have you happened to see them lying about?"

I kept hoping the whole problem would just disappear, but I knew that somehow, somewhere, my underpants would show up again. And I really didn't want to be around when they did.

"Matthew, what are you going to do for the egg drop?"

Allen was leaning toward me. His question took a moment to register.

"The egg drop?" I asked. "When is that?"

Allen looked at me a little funny. "It's Friday. She just said that."

"Who said what?" I asked, still confused.

"The teacher—you were staring right at her."

"Oh." I had been staring at the teacher, but my thoughts had been on the underpants.

"What was the question?" I asked.

"The egg drop, do you know what you're going to do? I've been working on a helicopter idea. I think it's going to work." Allen paused, looked around, and then leaned over. "I've also got a secret weapon," he whispered.

I liked secret weapons because they usually involved lasers.

"What is it?" I whispered back.

Allen looked around again and whispered, "I'm going to swap the egg I'm given with a hard-boiled egg!" He face broke into a huge grin.

The teacher was looking right at us, so we had to sit back and look like we were paying attention.

I had completely forgotten about the egg drop—one more thing that seemed to pile on the stress. Were we going to be graded on the egg drop? If my egg broke, would they hold me back a year in school? You couldn't take any chances with these big productions, so I knew I had to work on a really good idea.

So I pushed my underwear woes out of my head and formulated an idea. But I would need to get a bit more information before I made a final decision. And when I needed information, the really good kind of information, there was just one source.

Dad.

But I would need to be careful. This was one of those really great ideas that for various reasons my parents might not approve of. If I never technically asked for permission, they couldn't ever technically say no.

I decided to ask Dad in a roundabout way at dinner—a good time because it was very easy to change the conversation. If he started to ask questions that were too probing, I could always say something like, "Hey look, Peter is licking the butter again," and Dad would forget what we were discussing.

I was the last one to the dinner table, and there was a brief moment of silence while Dad looked around the table to decide who to call on for a prayer over the food. Peter was raising his hand frantically, but Dad called on John. I saw John stick out his tongue at Peter after everybody else had bowed their heads.

John started to say the prayer, and I closed my eyes. I could hear Peter breathing heavily next to me. He was mad.

"Please bless the food," John said.

Peter's breathing became quicker.

"And please bless . . . the water."

"Pot licker!" Peter blurted out. None of us knew what a *pot licker* was, but we used the name all the time. We figured that anybody who licked pots couldn't be too bright, so it became a nice variation on *stupid,* which we weren't supposed to use.

It was surprising that Peter had called John a name in front of Mom and Dad, but even more surprising was that he had done it during the prayer. I couldn't help but peek.

Peter had his eyes wide open and was glaring at John. John was still praying. "And please bless that Peter won't call anybody a pot licker."

That did it. Peter began to claw his way onto the table toward John, pushing plates and glasses to the side. Mom had already been moving forward and deftly grabbed Peter and hauled him onto her lap. Peter let out one more grunt of frustration and then sat still.

John, oblivious to it all, and never having opened his eyes, prayed on. "And please bless that there won't be an earthquake." He must have been reminded of earthquakes, what with the table shaking and the dishes rattling.

Usually after the prayer we all dug in, but we couldn't help but wonder what was going to happen to Peter. He had said a bad word in front of Mom and Dad, and he'd had the audacity to do it right during the prayer!

The prayer ended, and Peter sat still, sensing he may have crossed the line.

"Is it nice to call people names?" Dad asked the entire family.

"No," several of us mumbled. John was shaking his head.

"Is it nice to talk or do irreverent things during the prayer?" Dad asked.

"No," came the mumble chorus again.

"Okay then, just checking," Dad said. "I thought I heard something during the prayer, but since my boys know better than that, I must have been mistaken."

I was shocked. Clearly Peter had committed a violation, but he was getting away with it scot-free!

Peter sighed and then walked over to his seat. Simon started to grab at the food, a movement that seemed to break the spell. In a moment we were all scooping and pouring and obtaining our fair share of the meal.

After I had wolfed down enough food to satisfy my initial hunger pangs, I approached the subject of the egg drop.

"Dad, can you tell me about cornstarch again?" I asked. "What's that thing that it does?"

I could have been more specific, but Dad loved all things scientific, so this was enough to get the flow of information started. I could have just said "cornstarch," and it probably would have got him going.

"Ah, cornstarch," my dad said, leaning back on his chair to get into a more comfortable discoursing position. "Cornstarch is interesting for several reasons. It's made from corn, like a lot of things are. Corn syrup, ethanol. Oh, that reminds me." Dad's eyes twinkled. "Did you know that another name for corn is *maize*? So when you see a corn maze, you could call it a maize maze!"

He burst out laughing, and I noticed that Simon was chuckling and shaking his head.

"Maize maze?" Peter asked. "I don't get it."

"Well," Dad explained, "there are two ways to spell it. M-A-Z-E, and M-A-I-Z-E." Dad paused. "Wait, can you read yet?"

"Of course he can, dear," Mom said. "He's been reading since kindergarten."

"I thought he was in kindergarten," Dad replied.

"No, he's in first grade," Mom answered. "And he reads just fine."

All of this was keeping me from the information I needed.

"What about the cornstarch, Dad?" I said.

"Ah, yes. So cornstarch is used in all sorts of recipes, usually as a thickening agent. There is even a bit in powdered sugar, if I'm not mistaken."

"Remember when Christopher and Robin poured out the entire can of powdered sugar?" Simon asked.

"Yeah! They left footprints all over the house," Peter said, about to stuff an entire piece of bread in his mouth. "I wish I could do that," he added wistfully. He gave a quick shove to the bread and then sputtered, "Those footprints tasted great!"

"Peter," Mom added, "don't talk with your mouth full."

Peter, who was now trying to push mashed potatoes in with the bread, stopped and mumbled something that resembled an apology, but you couldn't tell because his mouth was still full.

"Let me see . . ." Dad kept going, oblivious to everything but his whirring mind. "I believe the reason they use cornstarch in powdered sugar is for its anti-caking effect."

Peter finally managed to get his roll and potatoes swallowed and said, "I like cakes."

Simon let out a large burp.

"Simon!" Mom said, "What do you say?"

"Ta-da!" Simon said.

"Simon!"

"Excuse me."

"But what about the thick part?" I said, trying to steer the conversation back to where I needed it.

"Yes," Dad continued, "cornstarch is an excellent example of what is called *dilatant,* which, simply put, means that viscosity increases with the rate of shear."

Dad loved to explain big words with even bigger words. I had no idea what he had just said.

"Simon," Mom said, "Eat your crusts."

Simon scowled. Dad kept talking.

"Basically, what that means is that if you mix cornstarch and water, and then strike it with an object or knead it vigorously, it will act like a pliable solid. But if you let it sit, then it becomes a liquid. It also does some really wild stuff when you put a pan of it on speakers and vibrate it, or so I've heard. I wonder . . ."

Dad looked like his mind was wandering, and since I still hadn't gotten most of what he said, I attempted a summation. "So," I said, "it can be soft, but if something hits it, it will become firm? And one might even say supportive?"

"Exactly," Dad replied, coming out of his thoughts. "And even more interesting is the use of dilatants in a torque converter. There is something called a limited slip differential . . ."

But I was already picturing my device. A box filled with cornstarch. The egg would sit in there and be able to move around, nice and safe. When it was dropped and hit the ground, the cornstarch would become hard enough to cushion the fall. I wondered briefly if you had to add water, because that would make the box soggy. But I was sure that if cornstarch had those properties after you added water, it would certainly have those properties before you added water.

Simon was moving a crust of bread toward his mouth, when it slipped from his fingers. It bounced off his shirt, and hit the floor.

"Rats," Simon said, a bit too dramatically, "Now I can't eat my crust."

Mom glared.

Dad was now talking about planetary gears, and I zoned him out and tried to scrounge up some second helpings.

Remember that I was one of seven boys. Seven hungry boys. Out of the seven children, at least three of us were in the middle of a growth spurt at any given time. This meant that my mom didn't just cook meals, she cooked entire spreads. She bought things in bulk, not only to save money, but also because it was the only way to keep food in the house.

I distinctly remember going to our grandmother's house for Thanksgiving and seeing a gravy boat for the first time in my life. We didn't use a gravy boat, we used a two-quart pitcher. The potatoes were always served in a huge silver bowl, and casseroles usually arrived in pairs. Only the vegetables were set out in rational servings since, unless we were forced, my parents were the only ones who ate those.

So I knew we'd have some cornstarch, and a lot of it. All I had to do was find the right bucket.

After getting in bed Thursday night, I hollered to my parents that I forgot to finish a school science project. My parents were both watching the news, but after convincing them that I couldn't do the project in the morning, I went out to the garage and found a sturdy shoe box. I located the bucket filled with cornstarch and dumped a healthy portion into the shoe box. I put the lid on top and then cut a little door in which I could insert the egg they would provide at school. Once that was complete, all that was left was to duct tape it.

After about half a roll, the box almost shined with the nice, dull-silver sheen of duct tape. I shook it gently and heard the cornstarch sliding around inside, and little puffs came out from the holes in the duct tape. I padded off to bed and was soon dreaming of the medals and ribbons I would receive for saving my egg.

On the bus the next day, I kept my box hidden in my backpack. After all, there was a small convenience store right across from the school, and I didn't want all the kids rushing over to empty the shelves of cornstarch, trying to copy my idea.

Allen showed me his contraption on the bus. It was kind of tubular and made out of an empty paper towel roll. He had cut lines perpendicular to the tube so that the egg would slide inside the tube. There was a weight at one end, to keep it pointed in the right direction, and on the other end Allen had fastened four propellers. He told me that the whole thing would spin around and float gently to the ground.

"Did you bring a hard-boiled egg?" I asked. I kind of hoped that he had, because there was something funny about sneaking in contraband for a school project, but I also hoped that he had forgotten so that it would be easier for me to win.

Allen scowled. "My dad ate it for breakfast."

School normally dragged on, but today it was especially long. There was some unwritten rule that if you were going to do something fun, you had to announce it weeks in advance so that it took forever for the fun day to arrive. And then once the day arrived, you put the event at the very end of the day. So not only did we have to wait until Friday, but we had to wait until Friday at 2:00.

Just before lunch the eggs were handed out, and we inserted them into our devices. We stacked our projects in the corner, and I noticed that almost every one of them had some kind of parachute attached to it. Didn't the kids realize that parachutes wouldn't work? Allen's and my devices were the only ones that didn't have a visible parachute. By the time we returned from lunch, the stack had disappeared.

The afternoon dragged on, but eventually it was time to head out onto the playground. We stood there, shuffling nervously, eyes staring up into the sky, necks becoming sore as we craned them first left, then right, trying to spot the plane.

We heard the plane before we saw it—a high buzzing noise. Then, from behind the trees we saw it burst into view. I had never seen a plane fly so low, and for a moment my heart stopped. Was something wrong? Was the plane going to crash right on top of us? The plane's wings seemed to be moving back and forth, and I wondered if there was a mechanical difficulty. But then the plane was over us and climbing into the sky. It slowly banked to the north and came around. I could see the door open on the side of the plane, but again it flew over us and continued to climb.

Let it climb all it wanted—greater height only ensured my victory.

Again the plane flew over, and this time it emptied its payload. One by one the contraptions were tossed out of the plane and began their quick descent to the ground.

As I suspected, the parachutes didn't work very well. Only a few seemed to be catching some wind and not falling as fast as the others.

One project, however, was plummeting to the earth like a cannonball.

In just a few seconds there was an obvious space between my project and all the rest. My silver bullet box left behind even the ones that didn't have very good parachutes.

The eggs were headed to the farmer's field just north of the school. My box had almost returned to earth and was hurtling toward the ground, becoming nothing more than a silver blur. But I knew the cornstarch would keep the egg nice and safe.

The effect was spectacular. The box hit the earth with incredible speed and promptly blew up. A small white mushroom cloud burst dramatically above the fallow field and then slowly drifted toward where we stood. There were screams and shouts from the kids around me, but I wasn't sure if they were making fun of me or just excited to see what looked like a small display of explosives.

"Whoa! Whose was that?" Allen asked.

"I don't know," I replied, pretending to look around at all the other kids.

But Allen didn't seem to be paying attention. "Look at mine!" he shouted.

At first I couldn't see his because I was looking at the group of objects that were now almost to the ground. But then I saw his spinning tube still very high in the sky. It almost looked like it was hovering, but then I saw that it was, in fact, falling—just not very fast.

"I think it's going to make it!" Allen shouted.

Sure enough, Allen's egg was the last to touch down. There were only four eggs that were intact, but his was the only one that wasn't even cracked.

I wandered around a bit, trying to take interest in other kids' projects. But in reality I was slowly making my way over to the part of the field covered in white dust.

It was clear my egg never stood a chance. There wasn't anything left. The box was dented and torn, and there was a gooey center that must have once been a perfectly fine egg.

I was a little disappointed, but mostly embarrassed. If people found out that my project was the poorly designed one . . . I would feel worse than I did now.

In my book, failure was bad enough. But if it was a public failure . . . horrible!

Several other projects had been torn apart at landing, and I picked up some pieces to make it look like I had a sensible project that just didn't make it.

The teacher asked a few kids, including Allen, to stay and help gather up the projects. The rest of us were free to go back to class. We started to inch our way back toward the school when the final bell rang. Like a herd of spooked cattle, we all kicked it into high gear and broke into a run. School was over! The buses were already lined up, waiting.

I ran in and grabbed my bag, and had just started to head toward the bus when I heard the laughing. Actually, more like laughing *and* shouting. I wondered if there was a fight, but then I noticed a bunch of kids surrounding the flagpole and pointing up.

I looked up and cold dread filled my stomach. In that instant, the mystery of my missing underpants was solved. There at the top of the flagpole, waving and flapping in the cool autumn breeze, was Yosemite Sam on a pair of briefs.

I wish I would have paused to think. I knew that the white cloth at the top of the pole belonged to me, but nobody else did. I realized later that I could have walked to the bus, hopped on, and nobody would have known. But panic had struck me then. I ran to the flagpole and tried to yank on the rope. I couldn't reach.

There was nothing I could do. My underpants were at the top of the pole for all to see and make fun of, and there wasn't a single thing I could do.

"It's not funny!" I shouted, close to tears, but my retort was met with laughter.

Defeated, I slowly backed away and hung my head in shame.

It wasn't just the kids from my class that were laughing. Kids from all the grades were heading toward the buses and sharing in a laugh as they passed. The whole school would glory in my shame.

A hand fell on my shoulder.

"What's going on?"

It was Simon. I couldn't say anything or I would surely burst into tears, and that would only compound my shame. I hung my head.

"Who did this?" Simon's voice had taken on a strange edge. He sounded mad.

I shrugged my shoulders.

Simon stood silent for a moment, then took a quick breath. "This was the work of the bullies."

I nodded slowly and quickly flipped up my hand to wipe my eye.

"You know what this means, don't you, Matthew?"

I shook my head.

"It means that the Hagbarts aren't working alone. Bullies as thickheaded as them couldn't come up with a scheme like this."

I looked up at Simon. He was glaring at all the laughing kids. He turned back to me. "You know what else this means, don't you?"

I shook my head again.

"It means we're at war with the bullies."

CHAPTER 13

I Wish We Had Some Blood

I sat on the bus, my face flaming. I kept swallowing because I felt like a baseball had lodged itself in my throat. I closed my eyes tight and tried to forget what had just happened. Having my underwear lifted to the top of the flagpole had to be the single most embarrassing thing that had ever happened to me! But Simon wasn't about to let me dwell on it. As soon as he sat down on the bus, he began talking.

"Okay, this is the last straw. It's an all-out war, and we have to plan our next move."

Still stunned from the events on the playground, I only nodded.

"Hey," Simon said, breaking into a grin. "Look at Allen."

I turned to look out the window. Allen, who must have gotten caught up in cleaning up the egg-drop projects, was tearing across the playground. Sunny was revving up the engine as if we were on the starting line of a major bus race. He had started pulling away when a few brave souls yelled out that Sunny had a runner. Sunny pretended that he didn't hear, but Allen ran right up to the door and started banging on it. Sunny slammed on his brakes, opened his doors, and let a panting Allen jump on.

Allen came down the aisle and held out his hand just before he got to me. I almost missed the fact that he wanted to give me five, but at the last minute I put my hand up, and he slapped it.

There was something uplifting in that casual acknowledgment. Allen continued to move to the back because he was the last one on. But I felt a bit better. It was almost as if Allen wanted to say hello, or talk, but since he couldn't, he just held out his hand. I really liked Allen, and in that small hand slap, I realized that in spite of the underwear incident, Allen still liked me. Allen never knew it, but his gesture had made the day bearable.

I turned back to Simon, and he started talking war plans again.

"Okay, we have to get them back, and have to get them back good," he said. "From now on, they're our mortal enemies."

The word *enemies* triggered something in the back of my mind, but Simon was still talking, so I ignored the thought.

"Wait, how did they get your underpants?" he asked.

I told Simon about the note. "I think I still have it with me," I said, pulling out my backpack. I searched through my bag and finally found it. I handed it over to Simon.

"Not bad," Simon said, "although they misspelled *principal*. This is definitely the work of the bullies, but I still don't get it."

"What do you mean?" I asked.

"Well think about it. Every time the bullies get mad at somebody, what do they do?"

"They beat the tar out of them," I promptly answered.

"So why didn't they beat us up? I mean, when they found out that it was us who played the joke on them?"

I shrugged. "Maybe they wanted to get back at us in the same way. Maybe they were tired of beating on people."

"I don't think that's it," Simon said, his brow wrinkled in thought. "They had the perfect chance to beat us up at Bear Lake. There were no teachers or adults near us."

Simon was quiet for a moment.

"Somebody must have talked to them after our first trick and convinced them to play a joke on us. That's why at Bear Lake they said they'd get us back. I thought they meant they would beat us up later, but they already had a plan. Or maybe the person helping them was coming up with a plan."

His logic seemed to make sense.

"The real question is, how do we get back at them? It has to be a really good idea. An idea even better than the one they came up with."

"Hey, it wasn't a good idea," I said, once again feeling the sting of embarrassment.

"You're right, it wasn't a good idea, it was a brilliant idea. They just picked the wrong guys to pick on," Simon said.

I was glad Simon was on my side. I was going to talk to him some more, but he looked so deep in thought I didn't bother him for a while. I thought, instead, about what he'd said earlier.

Enemies. He had said the Hagbarts were our enemies. I thought back to the lesson we'd had at family night. Mom and Dad had been pretty specific. So had Brother Winston, for that matter, when he had taught his lesson a few weeks ago. You were supposed to love your enemies. If the Hagbarts were our mortal enemies, like Simon said, then we were supposed to love them, not get back at them. I wondered if you could love somebody and still play a dirty trick on them. My mind wandered to the delicious thought of me beating up the Hagbarts, all the while shouting, "I love you," in an incredibly menacing tone.

"Okay, I have a plan," Simon said, interrupting my daydream.

"That was fast."

"Well, I haven't worked out the details, but I know our general strategy. We can't just play a mean trick right back at them. We have to do it with style."

"I like the idea of just playing a mean trick on them."

"Well, that's just what they'll be expecting," Simon said. "So we're going to do something completely different."

I waited for Simon to explain.

"They know we will want to get even with them, so they will have their guard up. We want to catch them unsuspecting."

I nodded my head.

"So we can do one of two things. We can either wait for about three months . . ."

I shook my head quickly. I wanted my revenge now. Somebody had to pay, and they had to pay soon.

"Or, we can play a small joke on them, one that's pretty simple. It won't be that bad, but then they'll think we've made our next move. Then they'll start thinking up another trick, and they won't be expecting us to do anything. That's when we'll nail them." Simon was grinning mischievously.

Simon was a genius. I would have just tried to get back at them, but of course they would be expecting that. This plan would work much better.

"So, what are the two tricks?" I asked.

Simon looked at me blankly. "Well . . . I told you I hadn't come up with the details yet."

"You mean you don't know what tricks we're doing?" I asked, annoyed that he'd gotten my hopes up.

"Don't worry," Simon answered. "I'll have something by Sunday night."

Simon wouldn't say anything else all Friday night. I tried to forget my underwear woes by watching adventure movies.

Saturday morning was filled with cartoons and our usual weekly chores.

After lunch, Simon, Peter, John, and I sat in the shade of a tree. Mom was in mopping the floor and doing a few other jobs, and she said we could either help with work or help by taking the twins and Jacob outside to keep them from getting underfoot. We chose the latter.

Simon brought out a book and lay down on his stomach to read. Peter and I lay on our backs, and after a while we tried to find shapes in the clouds flying overhead. John took Jacob and the twins around the yard looking for sticks.

Simon suddenly sat up. "Hey, Matthew, knock knock."

"Who's there?" I replied.

"Europe."

"Europe who?"

Simon started laughing. "No, Europe who!" He'd sort of said the last two words together, but that was it.

Peter and I stared at him. "I don't get it," I finally said.

Simon smiled. "That makes it even funnier." Then he turned back to his book.

Christopher eventually waddled over with a handful of dandelions he'd picked. "Mama!" he said, tapping me on the shoulder and holding the flowers toward me, his way of asking me to take them to Mom.

Mom loved dandelions, though we didn't really understand why. Dad had suggested we spray the lawn for weeds, but when Mom found out the dandelions would be wiped out, she said she wouldn't stand for it. She liked it when any of her boys would bring her a bouquet of the yellow weeds. She would stop what she was doing and put them in a glass of water or sometimes in her hair. In the summer we often had a centerpiece of dandelions at the table, although they were usually wilted and brown by dinnertime.

I took the flowers from Christopher and said, "I'll take them in to Mom." My reply seemed to satisfy him, and he plopped down next to me and grinned.

Simon looked up from his book and said, "Hey, Christopher, do you want to see something neat you can do with the dandelions?"

Christopher nodded.

Simon got up and came over. He plucked one of the biggest dandelions from the bouquet and then pulled most of the stem off. "Peter, come here," Simon said. Peter rolled over until he was next to Simon.

Simon put the flower under Peter's chin and rubbed it. Peter swatted it away.

"Aha! It looks like Peter has a girlfriend!" Simon said triumphantly.

"No, I don't!" Peter protested.

"The flower says you do," Simon replied.

"Wait a minute," I said. "How did it tell you that?"

"Look right there," Simon said, pointing at Peter's chin. I saw that the yellow of the flower had rubbed off onto Peter's chin.

"That settles that," I said. "Peter, you must have a girlfriend.

Peter couldn't see anything on his chin. "What are you talking about? Show me on Matthew."

I held my chin up in the air and let Simon rub the flower under my chin. I knew I didn't have a girlfriend, so I was safe.

"See, Matthew's got a girlfriend too," Simon said gleefully. "He's got yellow all over his chin."

A massive scuffle ensued. Peter and Simon were laughing, so I lunged at Simon to rescue my pride. Peter joined in, and after a few maneuvers we had rubbed a dandelion under Simon's chin. Now all three of us were in the same boat.

After the scuffle, I had to admit it was a good joke. Soon Jacob, Christopher, and Robin all had yellow on their chins, cheeks, and foreheads. Obviously none of them had girlfriends.

Simon lay back for a while and then said, "Do you think that's how the Indians painted themselves with war paint?"

"No way," I said. "They didn't get ready for war by going and picking flowers." I couldn't imagine anything so silly for the life of me.

"Well, maybe not the flowers," Simon said. "Maybe there are some cooler plants that give you color if you mash them up, like poison ivy or something."

"I think they just used blood."

"Whose blood?" Simon asked.

"The bad guys' blood," I replied. "From the war."

"But they hadn't gone to war yet, so they didn't have their blood."

Simon had me there.

"I wish we had some blood," Peter said. "Then we could get painted up like Indians."

"I can get some of your blood if you want," Simon said, grinning mischievously. "Then we could be blood brothers!"

Simon had previously explained to us the process of becoming blood brothers. It apparently entailed a person cutting himself and then mingling his blood with another person's blood. We had always felt that this was a good piece of knowledge to have, but so far no one had had the courage to perform the actual ceremony. Once in a while, when someone would get cut or scraped accidentally, we would talk about having the ceremony, but since no one else wanted to perform the other half of the ceremony, we still wouldn't go through with it. What we really needed was for two people to accidentally hurt themselves at the same time, but so far it had never happened. Usually, when the subject came up, we just concluded that since we were already brothers, we didn't need to become blood brothers.

"I wonder what else paints your skin a different color," Peter mused.

Simon and I looked at each other, and after a few seconds we were off searching through the weeds and flowers, rubbing things on our skin.

Nothing worked that well, and the whole subject was about to be dropped when John came across the black walnuts.

"This works pretty well," John said. I looked over and John had a decent-sized brown spot on his bare chest. Earlier we had all stripped down to our pants and had been smearing all sorts of things on our bodies.

Simon came over and we started gathering up walnuts. We soon found that the best method was to crack open a walnut, grind it up a bit, and then rub the powder into the skin. The longer you rubbed, the darker the stain became.

"Here, let me do your face," Simon said, coming over to me.

I paused. "Wait, you aren't going to paint something sissy on there, are you?"

"No," Simon said, trying to look offended. "I'll do some really good war paint."

Soon Peter, John, Simon, and I had stripes and swirls on our faces. Simon had given John a particularly great-looking handlebar mustache. We brought over Jacob and the twins and got them painted as well. The twins ended up with overexaggerated eyebrows and goatees. Pretty soon we were laughing and whooping all over the backyard.

The whole thing never would have made it into my *Book of Injustices* had it not been for Mom's reaction.

"Get that stuff off your faces this instant!" Mom yelled from the porch when she came to call us for dinner.

We trudged into the bathroom, and I got a wet rag and wiped my face. Nothing happened. Simon was holding a rag and looking into the mirror.

"I guess we'll have to scrub," he muttered.

Two minutes later, we realized we might be in a whole heap of trouble.

Mom rounded us up into the bathroom and began to try every method imaginable. Water, soap, shampoo, rubbing alcohol . . . nothing worked. Mom even pulled out some of her industrial-strength cleaners, but after reading the ingredient lists, she seemed to have second thoughts about applying them to our skin.

Dad was called in to help scrub, and the twins began hollering because they didn't like the vigor with which Mom and Dad were applying the rag to their faces. John stood in a corner whimpering frantically.

"Is this like a tattoo?" he wailed. "Am I going to have this on my face forever?"

Mom had appeared to be taking the whole thing pretty good when she suddenly stopped mid-scrub.

We had long ago learned to recognize the signs of a mad parent. Mom didn't do it very often, but when she became extremely mad, she stopped doing everything. She was at a point where she didn't trust herself to do or say anything for fear that she might do or say something she would later regret. She stood there in the bathroom, her face turning red, and none of us daring to say anything. Even Dad stared at her uncertainly.

Finally, after what seemed like an eternity, she spoke. It was in a soft, calm voice that made my knees weak.

"Do you boys know what day it is tomorrow?"

There was a pause. John finally answered, "Sunday?"

"Correct. And what are we doing on Sunday?"

John answered again, "We're going to church."

"Correct. And what is happening tomorrow at church?"

There was a pause, and since John didn't know, Simon finally got the courage to answer. "The Primary program?"

Mom got up and walked out of the room.

CHAPTER 14

Think of What That Guy Samson Did

Simon and I lay quietly in our beds later that night. Our faces were red and raw from where Mom had scrubbed, but the dark stains had refused to come off. Mom had finally given up and said something to the effect of, "Well, all those people who might have thought you kids are out of your minds will now have their suspicions confirmed."

Peter and John were asleep and the room was still. There was rustling from the top of the bunk bed, and Simon hung his head over the side. "You know what? I think I just thought of the two tricks we can pull off."

"What?" I asked, smiling at his wild mustache.

"You remember the first week of school and the ruckus Peter caused by taking a few of the chopped chicken feet?"

I nodded.

"For the first trick, we can take those and put them in the Hagbarts' desks."

I nodded. It wasn't the most brilliant plan Simon had ever come up with, but it wasn't bad.

"It won't be really embarrassing, not like the trick they played on—" Simon stopped as I winced. "But it will make them lower their guard, and then we can play the really good trick on them."

"What is that?" I asked.

"Well, it will take a bit of work and time," Simon said. "But I think we can grind up enough of those walnuts to make some powder. We can then figure out some way to get the stuff all over them. They'll be stained for days."

"You mean this stuff is going to be on us for days?" I asked, wondering what the kids at school would say.

"Probably," Simon said, and then quietly retreated back up to his bunk.

I finally decided to ask him the question that had been bothering me.

"Simon?"

"Yeah?"

"Do you think what we're doing . . ." I paused. It sounded a little corny. Simon's head reappeared over the side.

"What about it?"

"I don't know . . . it's just that we had that lesson a while ago, about how we're supposed to be nice to everybody, even people who are mean to us."

I thought maybe Simon would laugh at me, but he appeared thoughtful.

"Well, I think when they are talking about things like that, they mean bigger things," Simon finally said.

"What do you mean?"

"Well . . ." Simon began. "I think that would apply if we were going to do something really bad to them like burn their house down or break their heads or something."

I was quiet. I didn't recall anything that said you could be mean as long as it wasn't too mean.

Simon went back up and was quiet again. But after a moment he said, "I don't know. I guess we could ask somebody. But if it's an adult, they're just going to tell us not to do anything. Do you want the bullies to get away with what they did to you?"

"No," I said.

"Do you think they're just going to stop picking on us?"

"No," I said. "I just wish . . ." I didn't know what to wish for.

"Too bad there isn't somebody we could ask that would tell us to go ahead and get revenge," Simon said wistfully.

"We could ask a teacher at church," I suggested. "They're supposed to know a lot about this kind of stuff. And if they tell us not to do it, it's not like our parents telling us not to do it. They won't know because we only see them on Sunday."

"That's a good idea," Simon said. "Let's figure it out in the morning."

The next day, we made plans before church. Since Simon's Primary teacher seemed concerned only about enforcing reverence, we decided that I would press my Sunday School teacher, Brother Winston, for the desired information. Simon said that since Brother Winston had a tattoo, he might be a bit more open about what we could do to get back at the bullies.

For sacrament meeting we had a program put on by the Primary kids. It went off without a hitch—at least from our perspective. The adults were out in the audience, and they were smiling and even laughed a few times, especially when Peter stood up to say his line: "Our bodies are a temple, and we should treat them with respect."

After the program, we actually got a lot of compliments, and many of the adults gave us big smiles. I even heard a few people say some nice things about Mom.

"That woman is a saint. She has to be to raise that many boys."

"Patience that rivals Job's. That's what I've always said."

After sacrament meeting, we went to Primary with the other kids about our age. Since Simon and I were in different classes, we couldn't sit together. But if we planned it right, we could sit so that we were on the same row with only the aisle between us. So as we shuffled into the Primary room, we positioned ourselves accordingly, ready to discuss strategy.

Teachers don't like it when you talk during the scripture or prayers, but we found that during the songs we could carry on entire conversations. If you were looking over at your brother with your mouth moving, the teachers either mistakenly assumed you were singing or knew you were talking, but cut their losses and figured in the grand scheme of things, you weren't bothering anybody else. We usually sang close to fifteen songs during music time, so we would have ample opportunity to plan my questions for Brother Winston.

"So," Simon said over the tune of "Reverently, Quietly," the opening song, "what are you going to ask your teacher?"

I thought for a minute while watching the other kids.

"Well," I finally said, "we want to get even with the Hagbarts, so I need to find out if playing a practical joke on them is a sin that would send us to hell."

I froze. I had unfortunately said the last word at the end of a verse, in a moment of silence. Murmurs erupted around the Primary room. A few girls and several boys turned around with their hands over their mouths, as if to say, *You just said a naughty!* The chorister slapped her baton on the metal stand, pointed it at me, and gave me a cold look.

Simon waited until the kids started mumbling the second verse. "Nice timing," he said with a grin. Then getting back to the topic at hand, he continued. "Right. I don't think playing a practical joke is such a bad thing, but there is that whole, 'turn the other cheek' thing. Since this is a scheme to get back at something they did to us first—" Simon stopped. The children weren't sure of the second verse, and the sound level had dropped considerably. Simon waited until the chorus when the noise picked up again to continue. "Since this is a scheme to get back at something they did to us first, we need to find out if that makes it a sin."

I nodded. It seemed pretty straightforward. I glanced over at Brother Winston. I counted myself lucky that I was in his class. If anybody knew the ins and outs of the scriptures, it had to be him. Not only had he been on the planet for a long, long time, but the bishop had called him to be a Primary teacher. That proved he had to be some kind of amazing scholar of the gospel. They wouldn't entrust a class of children to just anybody!

Simon and I had to stop the conversation during the prayer, the scripture, and the talk. We would have to wait until singing time started to continue planning. But first we had sharing time. When I saw one of the leaders pull out a bag with a surfboard on it, I knew I was in trouble. I slunk down in my chair.

"Who would like to go first?" the leader asked. She'd brought this strange game with her when she'd moved from California. Nobody volunteered, which you think would have been a good indication of the popularity of the suggested activity.

"Jessica, why don't you come up and draw out a paper."

Jessica shook her head, but was finally coaxed out of her chair by her teacher and pushed towards the front of the room.

Jessica went to the front, reached into the bag, and picked a paper.

"Today in sacrament meeting, what was the opening song?" Jessica read off the paper. She looked relieved. "It was 'Count Your Many Blessings,'" she answered.

She was right—and lucky. She got to go back and sit in her chair.

The next victim was selected. Bill, a boy who was older than Simon, walked up to the front. He looked like he didn't really care whether he got the question right. He picked a paper.

"Who conducted the meeting?" he read. Then he smirked. "I don't know."

He had gotten an easy one. It was the bishop who had conducted. He must have known that, and yet it seemed he was begging for the punishment.

"You don't know?" the teacher asked. "Kids, he doesn't know. What do we say?"

Most of the kids hated to be up there if they didn't know the answer to a question, but we all loved to be part of the mob that delivered the punishment. In unison we all shouted, "DUDE, WHERE WERE YOU DURING SACRAMENT MEETING?"

It was really quite funny unless you were the sucker at the front. Bill just smirked again and rolled his eyes as he sat down.

There were ten more kids called up, and seven of them had to be asked, quite loudly, where they were during sacrament meeting. It was kind of funny that so many hadn't known what was going on, considering that we, as the Primary, had actually done most of the program. One boy, when he was asked who gave the closing prayer, yelled, "How should I know? My eyes were closed!"

We finally settled down. When singing time started, Simon picked up where he left off. He'd apparently had plenty of time to form more questions during the game.

"After all," he said over the tune of "Give, Said the Little Stream," "what we're thinking about doing isn't that bad. We only want to play a little joke where nobody gets hurt. A lot of people have done a lot worse. Think of what that guy Samson did. He killed two thousand Philistines with the jawbone of an—"

Most people call a donkey a donkey, but for some reason the Bible always used a word that you just don't say in polite circles, and certainly not in Primary. But Simon had made the same mistake I had. Right between "Give oh give, give oh give," and "Give, said the little stream," there was a nice spot where all of the kids took a big breath. Simon had voiced this alternative word for *donkey* smack-dab in the middle of this pause.

Where my mistake caused a few backward glances, Simon's expression caused an explosion. There were gasps from several of the kids who found the word shocking, and there were howls of laughter from other kids who found the word just plain funny. I've learned that all humor is contextual, and this particular word, said during singing time at Primary, was apparently hilarious. The chorister sputtered a few words, then banged her baton against the metal stand until I was sure either the baton or the stand would break. Teachers were reaching over kids, trying to get everybody to turn around and start singing again. Simon's teacher, a young man who had just gotten back from his mission, reached over and whacked Simon on the back of the head. Through it all, the piano player, who might have been a bit deaf, kept on playing.

Order was restored only after the chorister stepped forward, wielding the plastic baton like a one-handed sword. Seeing the chorister move into samurai mode, the children quickly settled down and picked up the tune.

Simon and I sang piously for five songs in hopes of getting back into the good graces of the Primary presidency. They were all very nice ladies, but sometimes I noticed a wild look in their eyes, as if they wanted to grab the nearest centerpiece and tear it to shreds with their teeth.

Finally, at the latter part of the song "Popcorn Popping," a song the children all knew and were singing loudly, Simon leaned over again.

"So find out why it seems the prophets can do things like kill bad guys, cut off arms, and stone people, and we can't even play a practical joke on a bunch of kids who would have been Philistines if they'd lived a few thousand years ago."

"I will," I whispered back.

Simon looked like he wanted to say more, but the last song started and was one that my brothers and I always sang. Whenever we sang, it was because either somebody was forcing us, bribing us, or because it was a song we particularly enjoyed. And, of course, the songs we enjoyed the most were the ones we had changed the words to. For this particular song, "I Have Two Little Hands," we had changed the words, but we'd also made up actions to go along with them. Simon and I both sang loudly, and if I turned the right way, I could hear Peter belting out our modified version from the front of the room.

"I have five little fingers on one of my hands." The Buckley brothers all held up their right hands.

"I have six on the other I don't understand." We now held up our left hands, but used our right hand to put an extra finger coming out of our left palm.

"During all the long hours till daylight is through . . ." We put both our arms up to make a circle, signifying the sun, which was the same action the other kids were doing.

"I have one little finger with nothing to do!" And with that, we stuck the "extra" finger up our nose and wiggled it. We all smiled as the song ended.

A few minutes later I was sitting in my classroom, waiting for the perfect moment to begin my questioning. We had gotten to know our teacher pretty well, and I felt comfortable asking him the questions.

As Brother Winston opened the manual to begin, I crossed my fingers, hoping our lesson went along with loving our enemies.

Five minutes passed before the topic was clear. Rats! It was on David and Goliath. I spent half the lesson trying to think how I could approach the subject, when I realized that I had a perfect opening.

I raised my hand.

"Yes, Matthew?"

"Why was it okay for David to kill somebody? I thought you were supposed to love your enemies."

"Ah, excellent question." Brother Winston smiled and looked out over the class. "Does anybody have an answer to Matthew's question?"

I wasn't sure if that meant he didn't have an answer and was asking for help, or if he wanted to see if anybody else knew the answer.

Nobody did.

"Well, that's a good question, but a hard one, too. Remember that David didn't go out looking to kill Goliath. He would have been much happier if the Philistines had just packed up and gone home. He didn't hate them. He was doing what he had to do to protect his country."

"So if you don't go looking for trouble, and people are bothering you, it's okay to get them?" I asked. That was perfect! All I needed was for Brother Winston to say yes.

I waited expectantly. Brother Winston paused, and then said, "When I was in the war . . ."

Susan quickly put her hands over her ears. Brother Winston often told us stories from the war, and Susan didn't like them one bit. I admit that sometimes they even made me a bit queasy.

"When I was in the war, I was asked to do a lot of things that I would never dream of doing in everyday life. We had to drop bombs out of planes. We didn't know where they would land for sure, but there was a good chance that they hurt or even killed people."

Brother Winston paused for a bit. "But I never did it out of hate. A lot of guys I know didn't want to be there. They didn't want to hurt people. In fact, we flew our planes during the day, even though it was easier for the people on the ground to shoot at us. We flew during the day so that we didn't accidentally drop bombs on houses. We were just trying to target the places where they were making equipment for war."

It seemed like Brother Winston was in another place, but then he came back. He looked at me, and I almost felt like I was the only one in the room.

"Let me guess," he said. "You're mad at one of your brothers, or maybe at some kids at school. Maybe they're the ones who painted your face in such a fine manner?" He chuckled. "And you're thinking about getting even. And you want to know if it's okay to get even, since it's probably nothing big. Maybe just a little scuffle, or a little trick to make them sorry they messed with you?"

I was shocked. He had guessed what the situation was exactly. I was so surprised that I simply nodded.

"Well," said Brother Winston, "I'm not going to give you the answer. If I gave you the answer, you wouldn't learn it as well as if you figured it out for yourself. Sometimes people forget that the whole reason we're here on this planet is to learn. And I'd rather you learn this little lesson now, when the stakes are low, than later when there's more on the table."

I had no idea why Brother Winston was talking about steaks on tables, but I started to have a bit of hope.

"So it's okay if we . . . I . . ."

"I didn't say anything was okay or not okay," Brother Winston interrupted. "I just said you probably need to figure out this answer on your own. And when you do, I'd like to hear what you come up with."

I nodded again, but before I could even form another thought, the closing bell rang. Class was over!

I jumped up and raced out of the classroom, taking off my tie as I went. My brothers and I had a little competition each week to see who could get out of their Sunday clothes the fastest—it helped if you were stripped down to your pants before you ever left the van for the house. Then you could run right in the house, drop your britches, and throw on your play clothes.

There was a brief period when a few brothers, who will remain nameless, went so far as to strip down to their underwear. If you were lucky, and there weren't any cars driving by when the van pulled into the driveway, you had the slight edge on the poor kids who kept their pants on. You could streak across the lawn in your tightie-whities and be dressed in your everyday clothes before anybody else.

But after only the second time (Mom seemed surprised), Mom laid down the law, and there was no more streaking on Sunday.

A few moments after class let out, I sat waiting in our van—my shoes, socks, shirt, and tie scrunched in a ball under my arm. I thought about what Brother Winston had said. It sounded like if we went ahead and got our revenge, we would learn a lesson. Dad always said that, above all, learning was the key. So really it was my duty to try to get revenge so that I could get whatever lesson Brother Winston wanted me to learn.

Simon hopped in the van, his shirt open to his belly button. "Well?" he asked.

I grinned at Simon and said, "Let's make our plans and get revenge. The bullies will never know what hit them."

CHAPTER 15

See How Bad It Feels?

Halloween night is when everything came together. Not only did we get a pillowcase-load of candy and pull off a brilliant trick on the bullies, but we found out who had been helping the Hagbarts, all in the space of about three hours.

It was my worst Halloween ever.

But in order to tell the whole story, I have to back up to a few weeks before Halloween. Simon insisted we wait a week to pull the first trick. "It has to look like we thought about it for a long time and then came up a with a lame trick. That way they won't think we have any brains. Then they'll lower their guard, and we can get them really good."

I didn't agree. "They aren't going to be thinking about it that hard," I said. "Let's just get them really good right at first."

"The bullies aren't going to think about it that hard," Simon said. "But whoever is helping them will."

We tried to brainstorm who might be helping the bullies.

"I'm pretty sure it's somebody from my class," Simon said. "There's one kid named David who used to get picked on all the time by the twins. And now he never gets picked on. And he's really smart. He's the only kid in the class who lasted longer than me in the school spelling bee."

So we waited a whole week. The Hagbarts teased me a few times out on the playground, but they never beat me up, and the week went by pretty normally.

Simon and I scheduled the chicken-foot trick for the next Monday, and for the first time in my life, the weekend seemed to drag on forever.

At church, Brother Winston asked me how things were going, and it took me a minute before I realized he was talking about the bully situation.

"Fine," was all I said.

Monday finally arrived.

I don't know why I was looking forward to the day, since the trick was just going to be our lame one. And it turned out to be pretty lame.

I reported to Simon on the bus ride home. "I sneaked the chicken foot in his desk, and he found it during math. I think it startled him, but then he just picked it up and made a face at me. Then at lunch he put it in my sandwich."

Simon nodded. "Yeah, the twins were about the same. They didn't have a reaction, and then they both threw them at me when the teacher was out making copies. One of them landed on Jim's desk and he screamed."

So our prank was a bust, but Simon assured me that this was all part of the plan.

"They're going to go back and tell their friend that we've played a trick on them. And they'll think it's their turn to get even with us. And while they're thinking, we're going to get them with our real trick."

"So can we do the real prank tomorrow?" I questioned hopefully, but Simon shook his head. "We have to wait at least another week so that they won't be expecting anything."

It was frustrating, but Simon seemed sure of what he was doing. "Besides," he continued, "we want to find the perfect opportunity. We can't just give them the powder and ask them to put it on their faces."

We spent several afternoons grinding up the black walnuts until we had several baggies filled with the stuff. It was hard work and made our fingers black. We left it to dry out on our windowsill, and I got excited every time I looked at it.

Simon and I were so busy planning and thinking about our revenge that when Mom asked me what we wanted to dress up as, her question took me by surprise.

"Halloween?" I asked. "When is that?"

"In a little over a week," Mom replied.

I always had grand costume plans, but when all was said and done, I usually ended up being the same thing every year: a hobo. It was easy for Mom to dress us up in some of Dad's old clothes, paint mustaches on our faces with mascara, and send us out to get our loot. It wasn't too bad because the costumes were relatively easy to move around in. I'd seen lots of poor kids out making the rounds who could barely move or hold their candy because their costumes were so dramatic. Or when somebody went as a basketball player, or ballerina, and spent all night shivering. When all was said and done, I'd rather be comfortable and warm.

Besides that, we had to wear our costumes even after getting the candy. Every year the elementary school put on a Halloween carnival that started after trick-or-treating. It consisted of a few games, a cake walk, and one entire room converted into a spook alley. Simon's class was in charge of the spook alley, and for a whole week their class worked on setting it up.

In the end, it was the spook alley that gave us the perfect setting to pull our second trick. I didn't want to wait that long, but I trusted Simon.

Simon's class not only built the spook alley, but they would also run the event at the carnival. There were buckets of peeled grapes that would be passed off as eyeballs, cold spaghetti noodles that would be passed off as innards, and corners where costumed kids would jump out and scare you.

"The Hagbart twins have a job near the end of the spook alley," Simon explained to me one day on the bus home. "They have to stand in a corner and pull on this rope about every two minutes. It opens up the exit. So most of the time people are just wandering around with no way to get out. Then they pull on a rope that lifts a curtain, and people can get out."

I nodded, but wasn't sure what we were going to do. "How do we get the powder on them?"

"It's perfect," Simon explained. "That spook alley is going to get really hot, and they'll be just sitting there, pulling this rope over and over again and getting hot and sweaty. If we put the powder on the rope, they'll get it all over their hands. And when they start wiping the sweat off their faces, they'll get it all over their faces as well."

"Won't they be able to see the powder?" I asked. "They won't wipe their faces if they see they have something on their hands."

"That's the beauty of it," Simon said, almost giddy. "They'll be sitting there in the dark. They won't see they have anything on their hands, and they won't see when they start to get it on their faces. It'll be perfect!"

There wasn't really anything we had to do to prepare for the trick. We already had the powder, so it was just a matter of waiting. It seemed like all of childhood could be boiled down into three situations: waiting for an event, participating in an event, and then being told that the event was all over. And as we waited for Halloween, Simon and I were on a high state of alert. We knew that since we had pulled a trick on the Hagbarts, they would soon try to get back at us. I opened my desk with extreme caution. I kept my sack lunches close at hand so that none of the food could be tampered with. Any notes I got from my teacher, or anyone else for that matter, I cleared with Simon. We didn't want the Hagbarts to play another trick on us before we could play our real trick.

We were successful—nothing happened before Halloween. The Hagbarts completely left us alone. They seemed to have forgotten the whole thing, but we knew better. We knew that they were planning something, so we'd keep a diligent watch even after Halloween—especially after Halloween.

Halloween finally arrived. I always felt a little robbed because I thought we should get school off. But when we got home from school, we dressed up and headed out to obtain some teeth-rotting loot.

Since we lived in a farming community, we couldn't just walk around and trick-or-treat. Mom had to drive us. She would come up with us to each house to make sure we had good manners, and to visit with each of the neighbors. Treats were always hit-or-miss at most houses. You might get a little piece of taffy or a handful of miniature candy bars; you never knew. But at some houses you knew exactly what you were getting. Mom had an aunt who always handed out slices of bread covered with cheese spread, pickles, and olives made to look like a face. They were wrapped in wax paper so you could put them in your sack, but we always just ate them right on the spot while Mom visited. We loved to eat them because they balanced out the sweets.

At another house the owners always had homemade root beer and donuts. We stood around eating donuts and drinking root beer until Mom finally cut her visit short so that there would be something left for the next visitors.

By the time we got home, our bags were full of candy, our bellies were full of sugar, and we were bouncing off the walls of the van. It was in this state that we ran in the house, hid our stashes, and then bounded back out to the van to go to the carnival. And, of course, at the carnival, there was more candy and pop.

Usually, when I went to school, I was there by myself—Simon and Peter were off in their own classes. And school was so regimented, you always had to be in certain places at certain times. You couldn't just wander around. But tonight I was with my family. And I didn't have to be sitting at my desk. I felt free—I could wander the halls looking at the different events.

As soon as we got to the school, we sat down in the cafeteria to eat our food, although with all the sugar in our stomachs, we didn't eat much. Simon had to help get the spook alley set up, and I asked him if he had the black walnut powder. In the excitement of the night, I had almost forgotten about our plan. Simon just smiled and patted his jacket pocket. Peter, John, and I spent the rest of the time wandering up and down the halls, stopping in at classrooms to take part in the games. I ran into Allen early in the evening and asked if he wanted to come with us, but he said he'd promised to help out some friends with one of their booths. I guessed it was some of his football friends, since he often hung out with them during recess.

I won a cupcake at the cake walk, and three cans of soda at the ring toss. John and Peter played fish and won a few trinkets. We must have wandered the halls a dozen times before the bell rang, signifying that the carnival was over. We ignored the bell, but eventually Mom and Dad found us, and we began the process of trying to gather up the entire family into one space so that we could all head out to the van and go home.

Dad had us stand by the kindergarten classroom, and then he headed off to find Jacob and Mom. They showed up a few minutes later, so Mom sent Peter off to find Dad. Dad returned, only to head off again to find Peter. Then we realized Jacob was missing again. Mom was mumbling something about duct tape when Simon rushed up. His face was flushed but he was grinning.

"It worked perfectly!" he whispered. "Come and see!"

He tore off and Mom hollered for him to come back. "I'll get him, Mom," I said, and before she could protest, I ran after Simon. We raced down to the spook alley, but the Hagbarts were nowhere to be seen.

"They were here just a minute ago," Simon said. "You should have seen them! And everybody was laughing at them!"

We heard some commotion down the hall, so we headed in that direction. Sure enough, farther down the hall we saw the two Hagbart boys coming out of the bathroom. Their hands were black, and they had streaks of black on their faces. The mess wasn't too bad, but it was enough that you wouldn't miss it. Their faces were wet from where they had been trying to scrub it off. They pushed through the crowd and out the door. They looked mad.

With all the waiting to pull off this trick, I had pictured this moment at least a hundred times. There were the black-faced Hagbarts, crying with humiliation while everyone laughed at them. I would slowly smile at them as if to say, *See how bad it feels? You better think twice about messing with me again.*

But as the real event unfolded, I felt nothing like what I'd imagined. There wasn't any sweet vindication. And I didn't really feel like laughing at them. I remembered how bad I had felt when the kids were laughing at me. I was mad at those kids when they laughed at me, and I was a little mad at the kids who were laughing now. I felt bad for the Hagbarts, and a little ashamed because I had helped cause the embarrassment.

And just when I thought I couldn't feel any worse, someone else walked out of the bathroom. He too had black hands and a wet black face.

It was Allen.

CHAPTER 16

A Spatula Won't Cut It

At our house we loved Legos—a few thousand of those little construction pieces provided us with a million possibilities. Every time you walked past the toy closet, you could almost hear the Legos begging to be built into ships, tanks, or weapons. We fought so much and so often over our Legos that Mom was forced to lay down some rules, the chief rule being that if you were building something or had built something, nobody else could salvage blocks from your creation. Too many times you'd spend three hours crafting the perfect star fighter, only to have it destroyed because somebody needed the red piece in the middle. So if Simon had eight wheels on his personnel carrier, we couldn't use them until he took it apart, a time frame that could last days, weeks, or months.

I had a beautiful all-black spaceship that had taken me a few weeks to gather all the pieces for, and I currently had several pieces that were perpetually in high demand. It was sleek and slim, and I loved pretending it was my space cruiser.

It exploded magnificently when I threw it against my dresser.

"It was Allen!" I shouted. "All this time, Allen has been the traitor!"

I found if I focused on my anger, then I could hold the tears back.

Simon sat on the top bunk. We had been sent to bed after the Halloween party, but I wasn't tired. I'd just found out my friend wasn't a friend at all. He had been helping the Hagbarts bully me.

"I can't believe it was Allen all along," Simon said shaking his head. "I was ninety percent sure it was somebody from my grade. But Allen is smart. I can see now that I should have suspected him."

I looked around for more things to throw, but then heard Mom or Dad down the hall. I grabbed a pillow and threw it against the wall, an action that helped me vent my frustration but didn't make a lot of noise. When I went to retrieve it, I stepped on some Lego pieces. The pain just made me more mad.

"I'm going to get Allen for this," I said. "I'm going to—" I didn't know what to say. One hour ago Allen had been my friend. Now I felt betrayed.

"We'll figure something out tomorrow," Simon said, lying down on his bunk. "Go to sleep. We'll come up with a plan to get back at the bullies, and at Allen. Although I still . . ."

I didn't point out to Simon that we had just gotten back at the bullies and Allen and that it was their turn to get back at us. And who knew what they would do? Would they decide that playing tricks was too nice? Would they go back to beating us up? Would Allen help them? I tried to imagine Allen hitting me. I wanted to hit him back, yet at the same time I couldn't imagine it. Allen was my friend. At least, I thought he was.

I didn't get to sleep for a long time.

The next morning, a Saturday, I woke up sullen, and my sour mood only intensified when Mom announced the day's activities.

"We're doing applesauce and pie filling today. I'm going to need everybody's help."

Mom was a professional canner. She often found good deals on fruit and vegetables, and then we would spend the day canning them. It wasn't too bad when you were canning food you liked, but I always dreaded the day we canned beans. I hated beans, and the days I would have to pick, snip, and bottle beans that I would never eat was, in my mind, the epitome of injustice.

I liked both the applesauce and the apple-pie filling that Mom bottled, but it meant that we had a long day ahead of us.

Luckily Mom had found a good deal on apples that had already been picked. Sometimes we had to pick our own food because it was cheaper. I didn't mind picking when the food was tomatoes, because if you picked a tomato and it was rotten, then you dropped it. Sometimes dropping it meant you dropped it horizontally, at a very high speed, in the direction of your brother. Those were good times. I'm sure that at times like that, Mom had to wonder about the benefits of bottling her own produce.

But picking apples wasn't that fun. There were ladders to haul, bushel baskets that were almost impossible to carry once they got full, and rotten apples that squished out mushy stuff all over your shoes when you stepped on them. So I was glad Mom had bought some already in the basket.

Dad brought in the apples from the van, and we were assigned to cut them up. We tried to make a game of it by seeing who could cut the most apples in sixty seconds. Then Peter cut his finger, and after he yelled for about ten minutes that it was going to fall off, even after it was bandaged, Mom said there would be no more racing.

Making applesauce wasn't too bad. You just had to grab an apple, rip off the stem, cut it into four parts, and then throw the pieces in a big bowl of water. Mom cooked the apples and then ran them through a machine. It was a magic machine, as far as I was concerned, and it saved us a ton of work. It pushed out the good stuff through a screen, and the bad stuff through a pipe. You dumped in the hot apples, and out came applesauce. The house filled up with the sweet smell of boiling apples.

The phone rang and Mom answered it. Whoever was on the other end of the line said something to which Mom replied, "Well, they're a little busy right now making applesauce, maybe another—" There was another pause, and then Mom said, "Well, why don't you come down here? We'd love to have you."

I wasn't paying much attention, but suddenly Simon was waving frantically to Mom.

"Yeah, you can just help us out here," Mom continued.

"What are you doing?" I asked Simon, but he ignored me. Mom got off the phone.

"Who was that?" Simon demanded.

"That was Allen," Mom said. "He's going to come over and help us with the applesauce."

I looked at Simon. He turned back to Mom. "I don't know if that's such a good idea," Simon muttered.

"Don't be silly. With Allen's help you boys will be done in another hour. Then you can play."

There was no way to keep Allen from coming over without telling Mom about the bullies. Both of us just stood there trying to come up with some sort of plan to keep Allen away. Mom looked at us and said, "But you won't have any time to play if you just stand there. Get going. The apples aren't going to cut themselves."

We trudged back to our stations. After a few moments, I leaned over and whispered to Simon, "Do you think Allen is coming over here to beat us up?"

Simon shrugged his shoulders. "How should I know? If he comes with the Hagbarts, we might have some problems."

I was a little nervous now. Cutting apples was one of the few times that we were allowed to use sharp knives. If the Hagbarts and Allen showed up, would Mom just give them all knives? Would we all have a knife fight in our kitchen? I had recently seen the movie version of the musical *West Side Story,* and I suddenly had a vision of Simon, me, Allen, and the Hagbarts knife-fighting all over the house, interspersed with singing, dancing, and quasi-ballet. It was kind of funny, but I was still a bit worried.

The doorbell rang. John went to get it, but I peeked my head around the corner. It was only Allen. The Hagbarts hadn't come.

"Hey, Matthew!" Allen said. He came walking in with a big smile on his face. He waved, and I could barely make out the black stains still on his hands. Was he showing me those stains on purpose? To remind me what I had done? I had to admit, he was a good actor. He pretended like nothing was wrong.

Mom gave Allen a knife and showed him how to cut the apples. I made sure to sit far enough away from Allen that he couldn't take a swing at me with his newly acquired weapon.

I didn't know what to talk to Allen about, but I didn't have to worry. Mom kept talking to Allen, asking him where he was from and what his parents did. She asked him about school and how he liked his new house. Allen seemed to bask in the attention.

Simon and I kept exchanging looks. I would glance questioningly at Simon, and he would shrug his shoulders.

We finally finished cutting the apples, just as the first batch of applesauce was finished. Most of it went into quart bottles that were then cooked in a pressure cooker. But some of the steaming applesauce was ladled into bowls, the best part of canning apples.

Mom brought out the vanilla ice cream and dropped a dollop into each bowl. The ice cream immediately began to melt in the hot applesauce. I took a spoonful of ice cream right at the edge. If you captured just the right spot where the applesauce turned warm and the ice cream had become soft, the taste was divine. If heaven was edible, this is what it would taste like.

"This is really good!" Allen said to me and Simon. We were sitting in the dining room and Mom was over in the kitchen, working the magic applesauce machine. Simon leaned over, squinted suspiciously at Allen, and whispered. "What is going on? What's your game?"

Allen looked surprised. "What do you mean?"

"Homes are off-limits," Simon said. "If you're going to get back at us, you have to do it at school."

"What?" Allen asked, scooping another mound of applesauce-covered ice cream into his mouth. "What are you talking about?"

Mom walked over with more applesauce and ice cream. We were silent until she left.

"Are the Hagbarts here?" Simon asked.

"No, why should they be?" Allen said. "I just hang out with them at school."

"So you admit it!" I said, a bit louder than I intended.

"Admit what?" Allen asked.

Simon pointed his finger at Allen, started to say something, and then stopped. He held that pose for what seemed like ten seconds.

Then he let his hand drop. A smile spread slowly across his face.

"You have no idea, do you?" Simon asked.

"I'm starting to have an idea that you're both crazy," Allen said, licking his spoon.

Simon sat back, pleased that he had finally figured it out.

"You've been helping the Hagbarts pick on some kids at school, haven't you?" Simon asked.

"Yeah," Allen admitted. I almost choked on my applesauce. He was so casual about it. Allen continued, "There were a couple of kids who were picking on them, so I offered to help them get even."

"We weren't picking on them!" I hissed. "They were picking on us."

Allen looked at me as if I'd lost my mind. "I didn't say *you* were picking on them. These kids at school were . . ."

Allen stopped midscoop. Simon was still smiling.

"Do you know the names of the kids you were helping them pick on?" Simon asked.

Allen's spoon dropped to his bowl.

"It's not . . . It can't be . . ." He looked sick. In a very small voice, he said, "I never learned their names. They said it was somebody in the fourth grade."

We were all quiet, and then Allen whispered, "Was it you?"

Our silence answered his question.

"But you had no idea that it was us?" I asked.

Allen shook his head slowly.

I still didn't get it. "But didn't you know they were the bad guys? Didn't you know they were the bullies of the school?"

"I felt bad when the Hagbarts got wet in the sprinkler," Allen replied. "The whole school was laughing at them. Why did you guys do it?"

Simon told Allen about the run-in with the Hagbarts last summer and the bullying during recess.

"I didn't realize they'd done that," Allen stated. "I didn't have many friends at school, so I offered to help them track down whoever it was that got them."

"So you told them to compare the note with signatures in the library," I said.

Allen nodded.

"That was quite brilliant, something I didn't plan for," Simon said.

Allen looked up. "You guys must hate me."

I didn't know what to think, although I knew Allen was telling the truth. He sat there with his head resting on his hands, his eyes downcast.

"Was it your idea to put my underwear up the flagpole?"

Allen nodded. "But I didn't know it was you, or I would have never . . ."

I was quiet for a moment, not sure what to say.

"I'm not mad," Simon said. "I was actually having fun trying to figure out who was helping the bullies."

Allen looked over at me.

I was speechless, but I wasn't mad anymore either. In fact, for the first time since last night, I felt better. I really liked Allen, and when I thought he had betrayed me, I was really hurt. But he hadn't betrayed me, and we were still friends.

I looked at Allen's hands. "Sorry about your hands," I said. "But look on the bright side. You'll have a new excuse when I beat you at Ping-Pong."

Allen looked surprised, and then started laughing, relief showing on his face. I had never thought about Allen being a new kid at school. He seemed so calm and assured that first day, but I could also see how badly he would want to make friends.

Allen and Simon went back to their desserts. Simon was slurping at his bowl when he suddenly stopped midslurp.

"Holy cow!"

"What?" Allen and I said at the same time.

"Do you realize what this means?"

"What?" I asked again.

"We are in the perfect position," Simon said. "The Hagbarts think Allen is still on their side. You can tell us exactly what they're planning."

Allen's face brightened. He thought for a minute. "Not only that, but I can help you plan something that will get back at the

Hagbarts! With both of our brains working on it, we can come up with a doozy!"

"And since they think you're on their side," Simon said, "we can get them to do anything you say!" Allen and Simon had both jumped to their feet in the excitement.

"We have a lot of planning to do," Simon said, sitting back down with an air of seriousness.

"We're going to need some pencils and paper," Allen said.

"Graph paper! We'll need graph paper! And a calculator!" Simon and Allen got up from the table and ran to get the stuff.

I stared at my applesauce. It was a beautiful milky color. My belly was full of creamy, fruity goodness. Allen was still my friend. We were going to get back at the Hagbarts, and get them back good.

So why did something not feel quite right?

Simon and Allen spent the rest of the day planning. I asked Simon how the plans were going while we were getting ready for bed, but he told me there was a lot of work still to do. "This is going to be the best trick ever played in the history of time!" he proclaimed excitedly. "It's going to be foolproof."

Simon worked on his plans all through church. I had been quiet during Primary class, so I was surprised when Brother Winston pulled me aside after class ended and asked, "So, how are things at school, Matthew?"

I shrugged. I wanted to race out to the van, but I couldn't just turn around and leave.

"Have you decided what to do yet?" Brother Winston prodded. "If I overheard you right, last time you were torn between turning the other cheek and following the example of Samson. You haven't been wielding any jawbones lately, have you?" He laughed at his own joke.

I shrugged again. I didn't want to tell my teacher that we had gone the route of getting revenge. The scriptures were full of people beating up on other people. We weren't hurting anybody. We were only playing jokes.

"Do you want to hear a quick story?" Brother Winston asked. I wanted to get out to the van, but I nodded to be polite.

"When I was first called up to go to war, I had to go to what they called boot camp. That was where they taught us how to shoot a rifle, get in shape, and obey orders."

I nodded my head. On Saturday afternoon they sometimes played old movies, and I had seen a few war movies where people had gone through boot camp. It didn't look very fun.

"Boot camp wasn't a very fun place," Brother Winston verified. "They weren't very nice to us, and we really had to work hard. One of the things they tried to teach us was a burning hatred for the enemy. They used to show us movies that said how mean and bad the Germans and Japanese were. They called them ugly names and had pictures that made them look inhuman. They told us stories about all of the bad things they were doing to American prisoners. They told us how the enemy would do the same things to us if we were ever captured.

"A lot of the guys in my unit started to hate the Germans and the Japanese. They wanted to get right into the fight so that they could start killing. They were going to war for the same reason I was—to protect our freedoms and the freedoms of others—but they were also going over to war with a hunger. They had learned to hate, and so they wanted to kill."

The story was making me a bit uncomfortable. I didn't want to kill the Hagbarts. I just wanted to play a little joke.

Brother Winston paused. He had stopped looking at me, and was instead looking at the wall behind me. I turned around to see if there was anything there, but it was just a blank wall.

"And then we went to war," Brother Winston said simply. "And we saw the ugliness of it up close. The ugliness on both sides . . . Sometimes, when times were bad, I would feel the hate start to build up inside of me. I saw the hate in others, and it was hard not to let it grow. But even after . . ."

It almost seemed like Brother Winston had forgotten I was in the room. But then he looked at me and smiled. "I don't want to bore you with the details. But when I was released from the military, I didn't hate anybody. And two years ago I went back and served a mission in Japan with my wife."

He paused. I wasn't sure I had gotten the point of the story.

"Some of the best people I know in this world live in Japan," he said, smiling. "Anyway, I just wanted to check in on you—make sure you're doing okay."

Brother Winston stood and started to gather up his things, so I left the classroom.

Out in the van, I stripped down to my pants. Simon was writing on some graph paper, his shirt and tie wadded up in a ball next to him.

"Have you gotten anything yet?" I asked.

"No," Simon replied. "We're just brainstorming right now."

I sat down on the backseat of the van and looked out the window. It was cool outside, but the van was warm because it had been sitting out in the sun. Mom and Dad sometimes talked a lot after church, or they spent a lot of time trying to round up all of the kids, so I curled up and lay on one of the benches in the van. I could hear Simon's pencil scratching against the paper. I tried to imagine Brother Winston in boot camp, getting yelled at by other army guys. I tried to picture him over in Japan, with a gun. I could see him, crouching through the jungle, looking for people to shoot. It seemed too strange because I had only seen Brother Winston in his Sunday clothes. So I could only picture him holding a gun and walking through the jungle in a white shirt and tie. Brother Winston was my Primary teacher, not a soldier. Why would anybody want to shoot at Brother Winston?

I must have dozed off because I thought for a moment that I was wandering through the jungle with Brother Winston. I knew I wasn't in danger because he was there with me. Then suddenly someone jumped out from behind a tree. He had a gun, and he shot at Brother Winston. I went for my gun, but then realized I didn't have one. Mom wouldn't let me play with guns, so she sent me to Japan with just a spatula. And now I needed to shoot the guy who was trying to get Brother Winston. "A spatula won't cut it!" I shouted. I hid in a bush and tried to see who was shooting at us.

Suddenly the van bumped over the railroad tracks and I jerked awake. Simon looked back at me. "Now you're dreaming about spatulas?" he asked with a grin, then went back to his writing.

My heart was beating fast. The person with the gun in my dream was Gil Hagbart.

CHAPTER 17

I'll Need Twenty Candy Bars

I sat on the couch with my *Book of Injustices* sitting open on my lap and waiting for family night to start. It was dark outside but still early evening. Winter was coming. When it was hot, we often longed for winter. And when winter came, we wished it would warm back up. But in the fall, we welcomed the cold weather and hoped it would get colder fast. Because when it got cold enough, the snow came. And snow in the fall was always a good sign of fun times to come—Christmas.

It seemed like Halloween was only yesterday, and here it was three days before Thanksgiving. To us kids, we judged the holidays not by what they stood for, but by what happened on that day. So Thanksgiving was really only a holiday in the sense that you got out of school and got to stuff yourself with a whole lot of food. But hitting Thanksgiving meant that Christmas was only a few more weeks away.

Christmas was the mother lode of all holidays. Not only did you get an entire week off of school, but you got candy, big dinners, and presents. It was like every other holiday all rolled into one, although without the fireworks (I planned on changing that by including fireworks in my Christmas celebrations when I got older). And since Christmas was the biggest holiday, kids anticipated it the most. Any kid would tell you that the weeks and days before Christmas were the longest weeks and days of the year.

Although the calendar said Christmas was getting close, we were still waiting for the first snow. The grass had turned brown, and every morning brought a cold, hard frost. But there had only been a few snow flurries. We still hadn't yet had the good dumping that would cover the earth with snow. When that happened, it would be time to break out in Christmas carols, start decorating the house with tinsel, and begin the final countdown.

November had gone by pretty quickly. With the Hagbarts under control, the bully problem had calmed down at school. Allen had planned a couple of fake tricks to play on us, which we, of course, avoided because we knew about them. And we played a couple of tricks on them, with Allen's help. Allen even let himself get caught in one of our tricks, a trick involving baby cereal and root beer. A few days ago, Simon and Allen had determined that there would be no more tricks until the final big one, which would take place at the end of the year. The Hagbarts would think they were getting even with us, only to have the whole trick blow up in their faces when we pulled the rug out from under them.

Of course, when I say "we," I really mean Simon and Allen. I hadn't been participating much in their plans because I found them to be pretty boring. They seemed to mostly talk, draw on graph paper, and test things out in the yard. I wanted to play, not plan. But they seemed to find endless joy in their scheming.

I also kept going back and forth in even wanting to pull the trick. Sometimes I would think about what the Hagbarts had done to me and my brothers. And what they wanted to do. And I would be glad that Allen and Simon were making their plans. But other times I would feel a little bad for the Hagbarts and wondered if we shouldn't just let things go.

"It's time for family night! I'm not going to ask everybody again!" shouted Dad from the living room.

"Good!" called Simon from another section of the house. "We're all getting tired of it."

"What did you say?" Dad hollered.

"I said I'll be there in a second," Simon called back.

Eventually, the family gathered and the festivities began.

There was singing, a prayer, and then business. After everybody had come up with some less-than-fascinating fact to report on, we started the main activity for the evening: the planning of the Thanksgiving feast.

It surely would have been easier for Mom to just cook all of the Thanksgiving dinner by herself, but every year she made sure to include everybody. And we loved to participate. So after business, Dad turned the meeting over to Mom.

"Okay," Mom said, pulling out her notebook, "I have a list of things that we need to cook. Let's decide who is going to help with each dish."

"I want the turkey!" Peter shouted. "And then I can eat all of it!" He grabbed the air around him and shoved it into his mouth, slurping and chewing with gusto.

"You don't get to eat all of what you make, Peter," Simon said from the corner of the couch.

"Well you always get to eat all of the deviled eggs," Peter whined.

Simon always made the deviled eggs because he was the only kid who liked them. It usually ended up with Mom and Dad taking one each and then Simon eating about ten.

"That's because I'm so cool," Simon said before going back to his book.

Peter was getting ready to charge across the room, but Mom deftly moved the conversation to something else.

"Dad will be doing the turkey because it's so tricky," Mom said. She was right. A neighbor had shared her turkey recipe with us several years ago, and we had never had normal turkey again. Dad had to cut the turkey open, remove all the bones, drop in a bunch of seasoning and a couple of cubes of butter, and then painstakingly sew the entire thing back up. It was a lot of work, but it was hands down the best turkey in the world.

"Who would like to do the yams?" Mom asked. "Remember, they have marshmallows on top."

Nobody said a word. It was one of the rare times nobody spoke during family home evening.

"All right, Jacob can help me." Jacob was too young to know that yams were vegetables.

"Yay!" Jacob hollered. "Yams!"

"Who wants to help with the cranberry sauce?"

"I will!" Simon yelled. Nobody really liked the cranberry sauce either, but it was pretty much just opening a can and plopping the sauce in a dish. Simon went for the easy stuff.

One by one Mom read the items on the list, and one by one we chose what we would do. I felt lucky. I had the grape juice/pop concoction, the mashed potatoes, and the candy turkeys, which consisted of gumdrops speared with toothpicks and candied rings. We used them as centerpieces, and then ate them with great drama after dinner, biting off wings and heads, all the while making gobbling noises.

Finally, each kid ended up with about three items each, not including the pies. Pies were an entirely different matter.

Several years back, Dad had declared that we would have only one pie on Thanksgiving day. Of course this statement triggered a rebellion. It's a good thing Dad was in a tickling mood that day because pretty soon all of the kids had jumped on Dad and brought him to the ground. We wrestled, tickled, and got tickled by Dad for several minutes before he told us that we should hear the rest of the plan.

"We're all so full after eating the big dinner," Dad said. "I think we should have one pie on Thursday, and then about twenty pies on Friday. Because on Friday we will have stretched out our empty bellies."

The reaction to this statement was much more positive than the previous statement. And while we never had twenty pies, we got pretty close. Everybody got to choose one pie to help make, and then Mom usually made a few more just for good measure. Every year we had more than a dozen pies, and then we would gorge ourselves on the Friday after Thanksgiving.

"I want candy bar pie!" Peter yelled. "I'll need twenty candy bars to make it."

"I want a cream-filling pie," Simon said, "but no crust or topping. I'll need several boxes of Twinkies."

I was ready with my idea. "I want a sugar-cube pie. If you take pancake syrup and dump it on the . . ."

One by one Mom steered us toward a more practical pie and kept track of each pie on her list. When the list was complete and tucked away, Mom turned to all of us again. "Speaking of pies, I have one more announcement, and then we'll have the treats."

"Who made the treats?" Peter yelled. "Are they good ones?"

"The twins were in charge of refreshments," Simon said. "We're having mashed-up broccoli."

"Are not!" Peter yelled, then he turned to Mom with a worried look on his face. He didn't want to miss out on his sugar high.

"We're having huckleberry o'cream pie," John shouted, which was a family favorite.

Pandemonium broke out. Mom tried again to regain order. After a few veiled and not-so-veiled threats from Dad, we settled down.

"Before we eat the pie, I wanted to ask you kids if you wanted to pixie again this year," Mom finally continued.

We all shouted, "Yes!"

The previous year Mom and Dad had decided to pick two families and deliver treats to them each night for the twelve days before Christmas. We started on Jacob's birthday, which was December thirteenth, and would drop off candy, cookies, or other treats each night.

We had to pixie in complete anonymity. The two families we had done last year never found out we were the ones dropping off treats. We loved it for two reasons. First, when Mom made the treats to deliver, we always had plenty of leftovers. Second, there was something thrilling and very spylike about sneaking through ditches, ducking under bushes, and delivering packages on doorsteps in the middle of the night—or rather, in the evening—but since it was winter, it was pitch black and felt like the middle of the night. All the sneaking felt illegal. And very cool.

"Who are we going to do?" I asked. "Can we do Allen's family? They're new in the neighborhood."

"We could do the Johnsons!" Simon chimed in. "Jared is my age and—"

Mom settled us down. "I actually thought we would do something different and just pixie one family this year. I know of a family who is having a really hard time right now. They don't go to our church, but I think they could use some Christmas cheer. Instead of doing two families, maybe we could do something extra special for this one family."

You couldn't exactly argue with that. We knew that we got a lot of fun things during the holidays, and if we made some treats and shared with somebody else, then that was a good thing.

"Who is the family?" Simon asked.

"You might know them. They have several boys your age," Mom said. "They're the Hagbart family."

My mouth dropped open.

CHAPTER 18

Ugly As Sin

The first few days of December dragged on. Christmas was in the air but still almost an entire month away. Surprisingly, the fact that we were going to pixie the Hagbarts didn't put a damper on the holidays. After Simon explained a few things to me, I felt better about the situation.

"It's kind of like a balance," he told me one night. "Playing our trick on them is not going to be very nice, but they deserve it. Now that we're going to be pixieing them, it kind of evens things out. It would be like if Samson beat up a bunch of Philistines, and then paid for their dinner."

"Really?" I asked.

"Sorta," he replied. "Plus, it's kind of like we're superheroes. By day we're plotting our revenge, and by night we do nice things."

But I wasn't so sure. One day after Primary class, I brought the matter up with my teacher.

"Brother Winston?" I asked. "If you're mean to someone, and then nice to someone, will that make things all even?"

He thought for a moment. "No," he finally said, stroking his chin a little. "It doesn't work that way. Once you've done something wrong, you can't take it back. There is no changing the past; it's set in stone. You should always try to be nice, but being nice doesn't erase past mistakes."

I nodded. Lying in bed that night, I thought about what he'd said. When I did something mean to my brother, Mom or Dad would make me say I was sorry. And I if broke something, I often had to fix it, or pay for something new. But that didn't change the fact that I had done something wrong.

With the bullies, our revenge was still in the future. If we stopped now, then I would never have to worry about fixing it. But once it happened, it would be done. And no amount of pixie treats would make it better. It would be set in stone.

I determined to talk to Simon and Allen about the matter, but then something happened one night that changed my mind. I went from wanting to let the whole matter drop to hating the Hagbarts more than ever.

It happened the night we went to buy the Christmas tree.

The day had been gloomy and snow was in the forecast, but the past weeks had brought so many weak and pathetic storms that we no longer bothered to get our hopes up. It was family night, and after a quick lesson on the symbolism of the Christmas tree and other Christmas icons, we all piled into the van. The fake leather seats were cold and hard, and we knew the heater wouldn't actually warm the van up until we got to our destination. It was dark outside and hard to see where we were going.

Picking out the tree was always an adventure, even though we usually just went down to the local convenience store and picked one out. It might sound simple, but it never was. Mom didn't go for just any tree—she wanted the best one. But that didn't mean the tallest one or fullest. In fact, none of us had any idea what criteria Mom used to pick a tree, but every year she swore that one tree always stood out. It "spoke" to her, she would explain. Until we found that one talking tree, we couldn't go home.

"Hey, why are we going past Jay's?" Simon asked. Jay's was the name of the convenience store where we bought the tree every year.

"We heard that the Hagbart family was selling trees," Dad called from the front of the van. "We thought we would go there this year. That way we can help them out. Plus, you can case the joint."

"Case the joint?" Simon asked.

"Yes," Dad said. "That means—"

"I know what it means," Simon said with a small shake of his head. "I just don't think anybody has used that phrase since the 1960s. Congratulations."

Dad mumbled something.

"Where's my angel!" John suddenly screamed from the third row. "I need my . . . oh, here it is."

"We're not really going to put that thing on the tree, are we, Mom?" Simon asked. John had made an angel at preschool. It was the ugliest craft I had ever seen, and that's saying a lot. None of my brothers were blessed with the gift of craftsmanship, and we had really come up with some whoppers over the years, especially during Christmastime. We brought home lopsided ornaments, clothespin reindeer that looked like they had some kind of disease, and snowflakes that looked more like they had been through a paper shredder than carefully cut.

But John's angel took the cake. It was made out of an empty toilet paper roll. Pasted to the cardboard were all sorts of things, most of which were encased in dried white glue. There was a wad of paper that looked like it was supposed to be a harp. There was some crinkled aluminum foil that probably served as wings. There was a flat piece with two odd shaped eyes—which were crossed—a large nose, and what was supposed to be a toothy grin. There were two arms that looked more like tentacles because they were so long. It appeared that the preschool teacher had emptied out the craft box and that John had affixed everything he could to his project, including beads, ribbons, and what looked like a patch of horsehair.

Simon had stolen the angel earlier and had run through the house making roaring noises with it. It scared the twins so much that Mom had to stop making dinner for a while to calm them down.

"That thing is ugly as sin," I said, grimacing as John made it fly in front of my face.

"It's a beautiful angel," Mom said, "and we're going to display it on top of our tree this year."

"That's why I had to bring my angel, to see which tree it looks best on," John said proudly.

Mom always put our Christmas creations on the tree, which made me wonder why she cared so much in the first place about the actual tree; all we were going to do was disfigure it with our crafts.

We finally arrived at an older house near the border of the next town. There was stuff scattered around the yard, including some broken-down cars. But there were about twenty trees leaning against the sides of the house, the fence, and each other. A man was standing on the front porch. He returned my father's greeting unenthusiastically, and then said, "Prices are on the trees."

"It's getting warmer," Simon said, looking up at the dark sky. "It's never going to snow."

I looked up too. I couldn't see any stars, but it did feel a bit warmer, and I could only barely see my breath.

We all wandered around for a while. I found a really tall tree, but Mom said she didn't like them too tall. "When it gets tipped over, I don't want it squishing any of my boys."

Dad went up on the porch and was talking to the man I guessed was Mr. Hagbart. Christopher and Robin found a dog and started chasing it around. I sat down next to the fence, but then my bottom got cold.

I saw Mom coming around from the side of the house. Apparently there were more trees in the back. I got up to look.

I noticed that Simon was hiding behind a tree. For a minute I thought maybe he had seen the Hagbart kids. But when Mom walked by his tree I heard him say in a deep voice, "Mrs. Buckley, pick me. I'm the tree you want. I will be a good tree and won't fall on any of your kids!"

Mom laughed, but kept walking. There was no rushing or pressuring the woman.

"Let's go look around back," I said. Simon grunted but didn't follow me.

There were more trees out back, but they all looked the same.

There was a shed farther back and I went to see if there were any more trees behind it.

I turned the corner and froze. Gil and one of the twins were messing around with what looked like part of a car. They were only a couple of feet from me. Gil looked up, and a toothy grin spread slowly across his face.

"Well, if it isn't Buck-Lee," he sneered.

I turned to go, but saw John following me. "John," I motioned to him, trying to make my voice sound serious, "go back to Mom."

John, however, kept walking toward me.

"Are there any trees back here, Matthew?" he asked. Gil laughed and looked at his brother, then said, "Just look around, stupid."

I wanted to turn around and smack Gil for calling my brother stupid, but decided against it. I tried to turn John around, but he pulled away, only to stop when he saw the bullies. I turned around to stand next to him.

"Hello there," John said. He must not have recognized them as the kids who'd tried to beat us up last summer.

"Hello, little boy," Gil said in a singsong voice. "What have you got there?"

"It's an angel," John said, excited to show his work to somebody who hadn't seen it. He held it up for them to see.

Gil snatched it from John.

"Hey, give that back!" I yelled. I wondered where Simon was. There were only two of them, and if Simon came, we would outnumber them.

"It's okay," John said. "They can look at it."

"I said, give it back." I tried to sound threatening, but my voice came out thin and weak.

The bullies took a few steps forward so that they were in the light. Gil held the angel up.

"This is an angel?" Gil asked. "It's as ugly as sin."

"IT IS NOT!" I yelled, now really mad. "Now give it back!"

John held out his hand. Gil looked down at him.

"You want it back?" he asked.

John nodded.

"Okay," Gil said. "But first Brian wants to look at it."

He started to hand it over to his brother, then stopped. "But I don't really want to give it to him," Gil matter-of-factly stated, "so maybe we should share."

And with one swift motion Gil Hagbart tore my brother's angel in half.

"My angel!" John screamed.

My heart broke at the sound. John wasn't screaming in anger or in terror. He was screaming in pure anguish. His angel, the angel he'd worked so hard on, had been torn apart right in front of his eyes. His dream of having his work sit atop our tree was now in two pieces.

Roughly five months earlier, when the bullies had picked on Simon, I'd snapped. I'd thrown logic to the wind and torn into the Hagbarts, motivated by fury and fury alone. I felt an identical snap now. I'd had enough of these bullies and their meanness and I was about to single-handedly beat the tar out of them.

I felt like I was flying toward them both, ready to swing my fists, when I was caught from behind. Somebody had grabbed my coat and stopped me dead in my tracks. I didn't care, I started swinging, anyway, hoping the bullies would step forward into my blows.

"Come and get it, you tinker toilets!" I said, using nonsensical, non-cuss words. "I'm going to beat the bribble out of you! You little libber pippins!"

"Matthew, that's enough."

It was Dad who had me by the collar.

I was too mad to reason. I could only roar in frustration. I took another swing at the air.

"To the van, Matthew." He was not to be argued with, but I tried, anyway.

"But Dad!" I tried to say, my voice almost sobbing. "They broke John's . . ."

Dad physically turned me and sent me on my way toward the van.

I realized John had been crying the entire time. I looked back to see Dad picking him up. Then Dad turned and followed me.

I was still mad. I climbed in the van, trying to slam, bang, and stomp as much as possible.

"My angel!" John blubbered as Dad put him in the van.

"It's all right," Dad said, hugging him tightly. "We can make a new one."

"No, we can't," John gulped, wiping his nose with his coat sleeve. "It's too hard. And we're out of glue. And Christopher ate all the blue buttons!"

"I'll help you," Dad said. "Now calm down."

I wanted Dad to get Simon, Peter, and me and go back and kick those kids all around the yard. I wanted him to pull a whip from under the seat. But he didn't.

"Dad," I started, "they—"

"Matthew," he stopped me, "it's okay."

"No it's not!" I protested.

"Shhhh," Dad said gently, although I don't know if he was talking to me or John, who was still wrapped around him.

John eventually calmed down, and Dad told us both to stay in the van. "Mom's got her tree, so we'll be leaving in a minute."

Dad closed the door, and I heard John start to cry again. I went up and sat by him.

John's was usually a classic case of little-brother syndrome—he would want to play, but we thought he was too little and would get in the way. But in that moment, I knew that I would never again think of him as a pest. It was my duty to protect him, and I promised myself I would be a better big brother.

"I'm going to get those bullies," I told him.

John sniffed.

"I mean it," I said. "Me and Allen and Simon are working on a plan to get them, and now we're going to make it even worse. They are mean, and they deserve everything they have coming to them."

"Really?" John whimpered. "What are you going to do to them?"

I had heard so many versions of Simon and Allen's practical joke that I had no idea what they were actually planning.

"It's a secret," I told him. "But when we get them, I'll make sure you get to watch, okay?"

John nodded.

I looked out the window. It was snowing. Not a light snow or a halfhearted effort. It was really coming down. I knew that in half an hour the ground would be covered, and in a few hours, we'd have a good four inches. Unfortunately we would be asleep in our beds by that time.

Simon and Peter were outside already trying to scrape together enough to form a snowball. The soft snow refused to stick together and would explode into white puffs as they tried to throw it. Nevertheless, they were shouting and laughing.

I huffed. Not only had the Hagbarts ruined John's angel, they had also ruined my enjoyment of the first snow day. But I would get back at them for all the times they had been mean to me and my brothers. As we pulled away from the Hagbart house, I leaned against the window and thought about how much I hated the bullies.

CHAPTER 19

That One Has Teeth Marks in It

On the way home from the Hagbarts', I resolved then and there that when we pixied them, I would spit on their treats.

But I didn't spit on the pixie treats for three reasons. First of all, spitting on somebody else's food is just plain gross. You shouldn't do it. Ever.

Second, although I was furious when the bullies had destroyed my little brother's angel, I had calmed down by the time we did the first pixie. If I had a plate of cookies for the Hagbarts right after it happened, I would have spit on it without a second thought. But now I realized we would get our revenge in other ways.

And finally, I couldn't spit on any of the treats because I really didn't help make them and didn't think about spitting on them until after Mom had already wrapped everything up.

So on December thirteenth, we started pixieing the Hagbarts. I found myself dropping off cookies, candy, and other yummy treats to my sworn mortal enemies.

Day 1

We'd learned a bit about pixieing from last year. It all came down to knowing what to expect.

The first night is always the easiest. In this case Dad pulled off the road just past the Hagbarts' house. There were plenty of trees and bushes around the home, so he was out of sight. We crawled through the bushes and over the snow. Peter crept to the door, put the cookies on their doorstep, and then rang the bell. By the time somebody answered, Peter was hidden around the side of the house.

Their mom answered the door. She looked tired, and almost closed the door without noticing the treats. But when she saw them, she bent down, picked them up, looked around, and then went back inside. Success!

Day 2

The second night is just as easy as the first since the target family thinks the first night was just a fluke—somebody was nice and dropped something off. They aren't expecting anything the next night. This time I got to take the treat. My heart was racing as I crept to the house. I felt like the door would fly open any second, and the Hagbart dad would come out with a shotgun. I put the treat down and knocked. I meant to knock four times, but as soon as I hit the door I started running. I ended up only knocking twice, but it was enough. I dived under a bush and watched.

Gil opened the door, looked down, and shouted out in glee. I was kind of surprised to see him like that. Usually when I saw Gil, he was threatening me. But right now he seemed like any other kid who was excited that he was getting treats for a second time in as many nights.

Day 3

Day three is the last of the easy days. The family thinks the first night is nice, the second a happy coincidence. But after the third night, the family sees the pattern, and it becomes hard to pull off the visit every night after that. After the third night, the family starts to watch for you.

Simon took the treats to the door. It was root beer and ice cream, and Simon positioned them next to the door so that they wouldn't get tipped over when the door opened. I could see his breath in the light over the porch.

He knocked fast and ran. The door opened pretty quickly, but he was already gone. All four kids were there at the door. The twins started to come outside. One of them was in his socks. Their mom called them back, but I could tell they were curious. They peered out into the darkness, trying to catch sight of the treat-bringer. They now knew that we would be coming every night. Now things got tricky.

Day 4

On the fourth night we took greater precautions. Before we left, we sat down at the table and made a map of the house.

"This is their shed and here are the bushes," Simon said, placing a few Legos on the table. Simon had even found a van in our Matchbox collection. "Now Dad can drop us off here."

"Wait," I said, "which one am I?" Simon had three little action figures next to the van.

"It doesn't really matter," Simon said.

"I want to be the bazooka guy," Peter said. The choice was between the bazooka guy, the radio guy, and the hand-grenade guy, but just as Peter had begun talking, I'd decided I wanted to be the bazooka guy.

"No, I'm the bazooka guy," I said.

Peter was in a bad mood. "I said first!"

Simon went to get another bazooka guy.

"Okay, Matthew, this one is you."

"That one has teeth marks in it," I protested.

"They're battle wounds," Simon replied. "This is the veteran bazooka guy. He knows more about bazooka guns than any other—"

"I want that one," Peter interrupted.

"No," I replied, "Simon said it was me."

It was inevitable that the planning session would end up in a fight, but with Dad's intervention, we eventually used identical pieces of macaroni to represent us, and we finished planning.

The first three nights we had delivered the treats at about eight o'clock. We did this to set a pattern. On the fourth night we showed up as soon as it was dark. The time change threw them off.

The Hagbarts were probably eating dinner or something because it took them a bit longer to get to the door.

Also, since it was earlier, John got to come with us and stood hiding behind the tree while Peter took up the treat. John giggled into his glove as he watched the Hagbarts' mom pick up the treat and shut the door.

All the way home, John went on and on about how incredible the whole event was. He told Dad about how brave Peter was to take the treat and how Simon and I hadn't made a sound.

I knew that dropping off a couple of treats on the doorstep wasn't that difficult, but listening to John describe it made me feel good.

Day 5

After the fourth night, Mom and Dad let us pull out the ski masks, which helped us keep warm, but also kept our identities secret. Plus, it helped add to the air of illegality.

There was some debate as to when we should drop by the house. Simon wanted to go early again. I wanted to go later. John said he wanted to go again, so we decided to go early.

Dad had been pulling off the road about a thirty yards in front the house, but for some reason this night he drove past the house first.

"Did you see that!" Simon declared as we drove by.

"What?" I said. I had been trying to look through the windows to see if anybody was waiting.

"There was somebody in the tree. I think it was one of the twins."

We waited ten minutes and then drove back by the house. Sure enough, there was a dark blob in one of the trees out front. We went home to wait it out.

We went back at seven, eight, and nine, and still the blob was there.

"Are you sure it's a Hagbart?" I asked.

"Yeah," Simon said, "it's changed shape."

At ten, Dad took us back.

"If someone's still there, you're just going to have to drop it off," Dad said. "We can't wait any longer."

But the blob was gone. Simon dropped the treats, rang the doorbell, and was safely hidden when one of the twins came to the door.

"I just came inside!" he yelled, but I could tell he was excited. "Who are you?" he shouted into the darkness.

I laughed into my coat.

Day 6

On the sixth night we pulled the "don't knock" routine. We put them on the porch, returned home, put a towel over the mouthpiece of the phone, called them, and said ominously, "Check your front porch." I always wondered if the recipients could maybe later trace our phone number, like they did in the movies, but they never did.

Day 7

Dad started parking farther and farther away, and from then on pixieing became a clandestine operation. Since we lived out in farmland, the roads were almost always empty. When we turned onto the Hagbarts' road, Dad cut the lights and drove carefully toward the house. Then we hopped out and walked one hundred yards or so to get to their yard.

Simon dropped it off again. I waited in the bushes and watched as he knocked fast and ran. Nothing. I looked at the house. There seemed to be only one light on. I waited. Simon sneaked back to the door and knocked again, then came back to hide by me. Still nothing.

"Should we knock again?" I whispered. He shook his head. We waited for another couple of minutes.

"Rats. I don't think they're home," he finally said. "We'll just have to leave it." We walked dejectedly back to the van. "Do you think some animal will get it?" I asked.

"Probably not," Simon said, throwing open the van door. "They weren't home, Dad."

"That's all right. Mom wrapped it tight," Dad assured us. "They'll get it when they get home. Remember how you were so excited when we found a neighbor gift on our porch after we got home from that Christmas party? It'll be the same for them."

I shrugged. It just wasn't as fun without the thrill of the chase. I consoled myself with thoughts of the next night's adventure.

Day 8

On the eighth day, Mom decided to take us. I had heard Mom and Dad talking in the kitchen earlier that night, and Mom sounded discouraged about something, but I couldn't tell what.

I was surprised when Mom parked the car and got out with us. It was a bit strange to see Mom on her hands and knees, crawling through the bushes. John had come again, since it was early. He sat in the bushes and giggled next to Mom.

"Keep him quiet!" Simon hissed. Mom pulled John close and whispered in his ear. Peter was the "doorman" and began sneaking up to the door. The Hagbarts were home tonight, but we went again at six, so hopefully they weren't expecting it. I noticed a small snowman in the front yard and resisted the urge to kick it down. I was in pixie mode, not revenge mode. Peter dropped off the treat and ran to hide with me. A minute later all four Hagbart kids were at the door.

"What is it tonight?"

"Peanut brittle! There's a ton!"

"I don't like nuts!"

"There's some without nuts!"

There was more excited chatter, and they looked out in the yard a bit. "Let's get some shoes on and go find them!"

I was close enough to Mom to hear her softly laugh.

We made a quick retreat, and were in the van without further incident.

When we got back to the van, I saw that Mom was crying. This wasn't a big surprise, because with Mom, tears often came pretty quick. It was a running joke to see whose Mother's Day present could cause her to cry the quickest or longest. Christopher and Robin usually won when they handed her small bouquets of crumpled dandelions.

"What's wrong?" I asked.

Mom smiled. "I'm okay." She sniffed slightly. "This is a lot of work, trying to make treats every night, keep up with you kids . . . but it's worth it, isn't it?"

I had never thought about the work Mom put into it. We kind of just got the fun part—delivering the treats.

"Yeah," I replied, "it's worth it."

When we got out of the van, she gave me a quick hug, and I didn't pull away as fast as I normally did.

Day 9

Someone had tied a dog to the corner of the front porch. We had heard it barking a few times before, but figured it was tied way in the back because it never bothered us. Not so tonight—it sat there, peering into the dark. I sighed. I was on my own tonight because Simon and Peter had been sent to bed early due to a fight over whether gumdrops were made in a factory or laid by the Easter Bunny.

I pulled up my mask to better assess the situation. I could easily get around the dog, but how was I going to get to the porch without its bark alerting everybody to my presence? I looked at the treat. It was a gingerbread house. I wished for a minute that it was raw steak.

We had a tradition of making gingerbread houses every Christmas. Like our school crafts, our houses always ended up looking more like condemned construction projects than actual houses. But we didn't mind so much because we knew that a few days after Christmas we could eat the gloopy mess. We usually pretended we were giant dinosaurs, attacking and devouring the houses with great gusto. It was my favorite after-Christmas tradition.

This gingerbread house was the best of the lot, but someone got a little too excited about the candy on the roof. It was an engineering marvel that the roof didn't collapse under the weight of the frosting, candy canes, a chimney made out of smaller crackers, a sleigh made out of assorted candy, and a cinnamon Santa. If the cinnamon Santa had had a face, I'm sure the expression would have been one of sheer terror at the way the sled was tilting off the roof. I thought about breaking a piece off to throw to the dog, but I wasn't sure dogs liked graham crackers. And I was afraid if I even touched the house, it would come tumbling down.

I was about to go ask Dad what I should do when someone suddenly came out of the house. It was one of the twins. He was grumbling, "But if we don't have the dog up here, how are we going to catch them?"

"It's not polite to catch them, Brandon," their mom called from the house.

He untied the dog and pulled it to the back. I knew this was my chance. Repositioning my mask, I zoomed up to the door, placed the gingerbread house on the porch, and ran back to the bushes. The plan had been for me to just run back to the van, but I couldn't pass up the opportunity of seeing the look on Brandon's face.

In a few minutes, Brandon came back around front. He was whistling, and then suddenly stopped dead in his tracks. He stared at the treats, then looked around into the yard, then stared back to the treats.

"What the—?" He bent down and picked up the gingerbread house. "How did—?" He stared out into the dark, then went inside, shaking his head.

I laughed all the way back to the van.

Day 10

On the tenth night, we dropped off sugar cookies. Peter and I took position behind a tree since it was Simon's turn to approach the door. He crept forward cautiously, but when he was about ten feet from the door, the porch light suddenly went on. Simon immediately dropped the cookies and ran.

The door burst open and all four Hagbarts came running out. I could hear their mother yelling for them to come back, but the boys ignored her.

Simon took off across the lawn and headed north, away from the van—our backup plan from the very beginning. The Hagbarts took off after him. As soon as they were out of the porch light, I stood up, grabbed Peter, and headed south. We would get back to Dad, and hopefully Simon could outrun them and find a place to hide until we could pick him up.

Only it didn't work that way.

Simon is short and incredibly fast, but me and Peter aren't. And while the Hagbarts were out of sight, they weren't out of hearing distance. Unfortunately, running across frozen, crunchy snow makes a whole lot of noise, and me and Peter had on our snow pants, which made a zip-zip sound with every step we took. As we made it to the road, I looked back. My heart skipped a beat as I saw that the four bullies had turned to chase us.

I was running as fast as I could, but every ten steps I had to stop and go back to grab Peter, urging him to move faster.

"Who are you?" I heard one of the Hagbarts call.

Hah! I thought. *Like I'm going to stop, turn around, and formally introduce myself.* I ran faster.

The night was dark and full of sounds. There was the sound of our feet on the gravel and of Peter huffing and puffing. It didn't sound like four people were behind me anymore. Maybe one, possibly two.

But they were getting closer.

What would they do if they caught us? Would they unmask us? Would they beat us up, or tell us thanks?

My chest felt like it was on fire. I didn't know how far we had run, but I couldn't see the van. I didn't dare look behind me for fear that I would trip.

Just when I was sure the Hagbarts could reach out and grab me, I was suddenly blinded. Two huge headlights had turned on in front of me. Was Dad crazy? He had just shined two big spotlights on us and blown our cover!

I turned to go around the side of the van and glanced over my shoulder. Gil and his two older brothers came to a skidding stop with their hands up to their eyes, peering into the headlights. They were illuminated in the white light.

Dad clicked on the brights and they all jumped. He honked the horn and they took off running.

Peter and I climbed into the van. Dad revved the engine and headed after Simon.

"Why did you turn on the lights?" I asked Dad. "Now they know who we are!"

"Ahhhh!" Dad said, and I could tell he was grinning. "You might think that, but in fact, they saw nothing."

"What do you mean? You turned the lights right on me."

"Yes, but you were between them and the lights. All they would have seen is your silhouettes. Trust me, they saw nothing."

Dad drove until he saw Simon standing on the side of the road and waving. I opened the door and Simon got in. Dad did a quick U-turn.

"My goodness," Dad said, "that was tense there for a moment."

"Yeah," Simon said, pulling off his ski mask. "That was close."

"You must feel like Sir Edmund Hillary when he climbed Mt. Everest for the first time."

We went silent, confused.

"What?" Simon asked after a moment. "What are you talking about?"

"Well it was a Tensing situation!" Dad said, laughing. "Get it? Everest! Hillary! Tensing!" Somehow I think Dad got more pleasure out of jokes we didn't understand than the ones we got.

When we got home, Simon and I went straight to the encyclopedia to try to figure out Dad's joke.

CHAPTER 20

The Future Can Be Changed

Day 11

It was December twenty-third. School was finally over for the holiday break, and we couldn't have been happier. There was only Christmas Eve left before it was glorious Christmas morning. Then followed an entire week of vacation that consisted of sleeping in, playing with our new toys, and hanging around telling Mom how bored we were.

Speaking of toys, we had been poring over toy catalogs for weeks now, making up new lists for Santa every few hours. Simon told us that Santa had everything in his bag, so you could leave a new list on the dining room table, and he'd see it when he came. For some reason, this seemed to cause Mom and Dad a lot of stress.

Mom saw us looking at all the toys. "Remember boys," she said, "it's better to give than to receive."

"Is that right?" I asked Simon. "I've heard that before, but I'm not sure what it means. I think it's better to get."

"Yeah," Simon said, "I've tried to figure that out too. I think maybe it's a saying made up by the toy makers, because either way they come out ahead."

Allen came over and played after school let out. He had been coming over to our house a lot lately as he and Simon made up their final plans. They were keeping them in a manila envelope—for safety reasons, they said.

"When do I get to find out what they are?" I asked. "I want to help." I reminded myself every day what the Hagbarts had done to John, and I was eager for revenge.

"We'll tell you tonight," Simon said. "Allen wants to come and pixie with us. We'll talk about it then."

"You told Allen about pixieing the Hagbarts?" I asked, incredulous. That was letting out our biggest secret!

Simon shrugged. "He won't tell anybody."

Allen went home for dinner, and we had ours. After the dishes were cleaned up, Dad took Simon and me out to pixie. We swung by to pick up Allen.

Dad dropped all three of us off well away from the house. Instead of walking along the road, we cut into one of the fields to approach the house from the back. It was my turn to go to the door, but I was a bit nervous after last night, so I decided to let Simon take the paper plate of homemade candy to the door.

"So what are we going to do tomorrow?" I asked as we walked to the house. "To the Hagbarts?"

Simon laughed softly. Bit by bit, he and Allen explained the plan. At first I couldn't believe it.

"That sounds so simple! What happened to the exploding watermelons? Or the camera crew? Or the high-pressured applesauce shooter?" I wondered aloud. "I know you at least mentioned some of that before."

Allen shook his head. "Too complicated."

Simon agreed. "In all of our planning, Allen and I found that the simpler it is, the more likely it will work."

I thought about it for a moment and slowly smiled. The plan was good, and while I wondered about how they were going to pull off some of the slightly more complicated aspects, this plan was, on the whole, plain and simple. And completely possible.

We sneaked up to the back of the house and then hid behind the shed. I shivered a little. We were on the same spot where John had had his angel torn in two.

"You stay hidden, and I'll drop off the stuff," Simon told me and Allen. "If they chase me, just stay still until they're back in the house."

"I want to come," Allen said, sounding excited. "Are you sure this isn't illegal?"

"It's legal," Simon reassured Allen. "We aren't breaking or taking anything. We're not even entering their house."

"Oh," said Allen, sounding a little disappointed.

"Will you be okay here, Matthew?" Simon asked.

I nodded in the darkness. "Yeah, I'll wait here, and then either sneak to the road or go back the way we came."

I watched as Simon and Allen crept around the side of the house. I could picture what Simon was doing up front. He would get on all fours so anybody looking out the window wouldn't see him. Allen would be following, probably whispering excitedly until Simon looked back and shushed him. Then Simon would put the food down, and they would both knock.

The porch light came on, and when I craned my neck around the corner of the shed, I could see Simon and Allen sprinting across the front lawn. Two of the Hagbarts were chasing them, but it was clear they wouldn't catch either one. Allen was running even faster than Simon, and was yelling like a goon. I smiled. I would wait here, and then sneak back around after they . . .

One of the Hagbarts wasn't going back into the house. He was headed into the backyard. Back toward me.

It was Gil.

I whipped my head back around the shed and held my breath. He couldn't have seen me. I was sitting in pitch darkness. And I hadn't made a sound.

Gil stopped in the middle of the yard. He was only about twenty feet from me, but he hadn't seen me; he was just hanging out in his backyard. I considered my options.

I didn't have any.

It was a cold night, and the snow was crunchy. If I moved an inch Gil would certainly hear me. I was trapped. I didn't even dare breathe.

This was very bad.

"Here boy!" Gil called. "Come and see Gil."

I heard a dog come shuffling from somewhere.

"Good boy," Gil said. "You're a good dog."

I remembered my surprise from the other day at hearing Gil sound like just a normal kid. I was used to Gil talking mean to me or to the other kids. But now he was just a kid, talking to his dog. But then I reminded myself of what he had done to John, and I could feel the anger building up in me again.

There was nothing to do but wait, and nothing to do while I waited except think. I thought about the plan Simon and Allen had just described to me. I closed my eyes and tried to picture the entire event: By sundown tomorrow, the entire town would be convinced that the Hagbarts were thieves.

Every year on Christmas Eve, our church held a celebration for the entire neighborhood. It started around four, and there were games and activities. Dinner was served, and then everyone was gathered up to sing Christmas carols. After a few songs we would sing "Here Comes Santa Claus," and lo and behold, who should appear but Santa himself, carrying little bags filled with candy canes, peanuts, a few pieces of chocolate, and an orange. You had to sit on Santa's lap to get the bag of treats.

Along with all the activities was a big jar filled with money that sat on the main table. Everybody donated what he or she could, and then the money was given to the local food bank. Mom and Dad usually had us do a few odd "money" jobs on Christmas Eve morning. This not only kept us from whining about how long the day was, but helped us earn some money to put in the jar that night.

Nobody really watched the money, because nobody would be so low as to steal money from the hungry and needy. So nobody would notice if a few decorations were missing from around the jar, either.

I opened my eyes and saw our van drive slowly by the Hagbart house. Dad would be wondering where I was. But what else could I do? I didn't think I could outrun Gil.

Gil was still petting his dog and talking to it. I could hear some slobber noises and guessed that the dog was licking Gil's face.

I heard loud voices coming from inside the house. I couldn't understand what they were saying, but somebody sounded mad. I closed my eyes and went back to imagining the next night's event.

Santa usually had two older kids helping him to hand out the candy, and Allen would volunteer to be one of those kids. He would hand out the bags as kids came and sat on Santa's lap.

The beauty of the plan lay in the fact that the Hagbarts thought they were working with Allen to play a trick on us. But Allen and Simon would actually turn that trick back on the Hagbarts.

The Hagbarts would sit on Santa's lap and get one of Santa's bags. They would then take these bags, write the name "Buckley" on them, and put money inside them—the Hagbarts had been saving for three weeks.

After the Hagbarts went through the line, we would go through and sit on Santa's lap. We would get just regular bags, eat all the good stuff, and place the remaining candy in our pockets—then go after the "evidence."

Every year the tables were decorated with lots of little trinkets. Nothing fancy or valuable, but stuff borrowed from other people to make the tables look nicer. After we had emptied our bags of the candy, we would "borrow" a few of these trinkets and place them in our bags. Simon had a marker, and we would write "Hagbart" on the inside of each bag.

So we had the bags labeled "Hagbart," and they had the bags with "Buckley" on them. The "Buckley" bags had money in them, and the "Hagbart" bags had stolen decorations.

We would then put the bags by our coats, out in the hall where nobody would be watching them—except the Hagbarts.

My thoughts were interrupted by yelling coming from inside the Hagbart house and so I opened my eyes. At my house there was always yelling. In fact, it was strange when it was quiet. But this yelling wasn't like at my house. This yelling sounded very loud, very mad, and very deep.

It was Gil's dad.

I was on all fours, so I leaned forward and looked around the corner of the shed. The back door flew open, and I saw Gil jump. He was still sitting by his dog, but he spun so he could face his dad.

"What in the—?" The Hagbarts' dad sounded weird and he talked with a slur. "Why are you sitting out here in the cold like an idiot?"

I took a sharp breath. His dad's voice sounded full of hate. I had never heard my dad talk like that to anybody, let alone to me or one of my brothers.

"What did I tell you about that stupid dog?" his dad said. The dog whimpered. Gil's dad had walked over to stand by his son and the dog. I thought maybe they both would start laughing. Maybe this was some kind of weird joke they both shared.

Gil's dad suddenly kicked at the dog. He missed, but the dog tore across the yard anyway, yelping and howling.

I closed my eyes. I wanted to shut out the scene in front of me. But I couldn't shut out the sounds. I was scared.

"Dad!" Gil sounded scared. Scared of his own dad.

"Stand up," I heard his dad order.

I opened my eyes.

Gil stood up slowly.

"Why didn't you shovel the walk like I asked?"

Both my dad and my mom asked me this question at least ten times after a snowstorm, but not like this.

"You're worthless," he said. "You're nothing but a . . ." Gil's dad used a word I had never heard before, and I decided right then and there that I never wanted to hear it again. It was an ugly, ugly word.

"I am not!" Gil yelled.

I was panicked, and I couldn't tell for sure what was happening. I wasn't sure if he pushed Gil or if he just stumbled and bumped against him, but either way, Gil fell backward.

I wanted to run. To get away from there as fast as I could. I wanted to close my eyes and make the scene disappear. I wanted somebody to come and stop this. But I couldn't move because they would both hear me.

I saw Gil's dad step closer, and then I couldn't watch anymore. I dug my head into my coat, and willed for him to stop. None of this was happening. I couldn't see it, so it wasn't happening.

But when I closed my eyes, I couldn't help but see the scene at tomorrow's party. I saw it like it had already happened.

Our bags, the ones with the name Hagbart on them, were out in the hall, where nobody was watching. The decorations from the table were inside. The Hagbarts would sneak into the coatroom and trade their bags with our bags. So now our bags had money in them, and their bags had the trinkets, buried under a pile of peanuts.

The Hagbarts would come back into the main hall and give Allen the signal, which, of course, we would be watching for—a quick brush of the hand through their hair.

Simon would slip out, empty the money from all of the bags, put our old candy back in, put the money in the big jar, and then give Allen another signal—a thumbs-up.

Our bags now held nothing but candy, and the Hagbarts' bags held the trinkets taken from the tables.

At this point, Allen would find the Hagbarts and tell them to make their accusation.

There was a sickness in my stomach, and my chest felt tight. I didn't want to watch what would happen if we played the trick, but with my eyes closed, it wouldn't stop.

And with what was happening ten feet away, I couldn't open my eyes either.

I buried my head deeper into my coat. The Hagbarts would go to one of the adults in charge and tell them that they saw us taking money from the donation jar and putting it in our sacks. Of course there would be an uproar. Our parents would be called over and the entire community would overhear that the Buckley boys had taken money from the jar that was for the poor!

And, of course, our bags would be searched and would contain only candy.

Then Simon, with an incredible amount of piety, would say that we never took the money. In fact, he had been standing guard over the money jar because he saw the Hagbarts taking some of the decorations from the table and hiding them in their bags. He didn't want them taking the money, too.

And then the attention would be turned on the Hagbart boys and their bags would be inspected. The decorations would be found, and sweet revenge would be ours. The Hagbarts would be humiliated. I could see it as clear as anything. I knew it would work. I could picture it now, Gil kneeling on the floor on the church gym, crying because he felt so bad.

But I wasn't just imagining it. Gil was, in fact, crying. I opened my eyes, and saw him alone in the snow, sobbing softly. His dad had gone back into the house.

I wanted to throw up.

His dog came over, and for a minute Gil held him. Then suddenly he pushed the dog away. "You're worthless!" he shouted at his dog, who yelped and ran away again.

I was crying, too. The cold made my wet cheeks even colder. I wanted to help Gil. I wanted to change what had just happened, to go back in time. I felt like I had caused part of his hurt. I wanted to take back all the mean things I had done and make them right. But I remembered what Brother Winston said. The past is set in stone.

Thinking of Brother Winston suddenly brought something into focus. I felt I was looking at Gil with a new pair of glasses. He wasn't a bully. He was a little kid, just like me. A kid who was in a rough spot and needed friends, not people playing mean tricks on him. What in the world was I thinking? Why had I ever wanted to get revenge?

Gil had been mean to me. Gil and his brothers had bullied me and my brothers. And yet I was no longer mad. I no longer wanted revenge. How could I possibly want to keep hurting this kid crying in the snow? I felt sick for ever wanting to. What if we had already pulled our prank? What if we had already hurt him and his brothers? What would his dad have done if they had been caught with those decorations in their bags?

But we hadn't. The prank was still in the future, and the future could be changed.

I knew in that moment that Simon, Allen, and I couldn't get even. I understood why the Hagbarts acted mean now—because they were treated mean and were taught to be mean. And it made me feel sad. My hate was gone. I even thought of John and his angel being torn apart by Gil. But it didn't make a difference. When John needed help, Dad was there to comfort him and to hold him. What Gil had done was mean, but I could forgive him.

I saw the van slowly drive by again. A few moments later Gil got up and went into the house. I stood up and ran out to the road.

"What happened?" Simon asked me when I got in the van. I couldn't speak. My insides felt like they were tied up. I just shook my head.

"Where were you?" Simon asked again. "Did they catch you?"

I shook my head again. If I said anything, I knew I'd burst out crying.

"So what happened?"

Dad saved me.

"Are you okay, Matthew?" he asked quietly.

I nodded.

"Simon," Dad said, "he's okay. We can talk about it later."

CHAPTER 21

Just an Old Man

It was finally Christmas Eve.

It was an eventful day. The night before Dad and Mom had called me into their bedroom after we'd all been sent to bed. They asked me what had happened at the Hagbarts'.

I couldn't talk. I just stared at them, wishing I could forget everything I had seen. Mom put her arms around me. "It's okay," she soothed.

It took me a while, but in the end, I told them. I explained that Gil's dad had called him names and pushed him down. As I cried, they held me and told me that everything would work out.

"That family has been going through some really rough times," Mom said. "That was one of the reasons why I thought it would be a good idea to pixie them."

I nodded. If we hadn't pixied them, I never would have seen that other side of Gil, and we would have gone through with our prank. I went to bed feeling a little better.

Then, a few hours before the party, Simon and I went down to Allen's house. We played for just a bit. I don't know if it was because I was preoccupied with my thoughts or because Allen had finally gotten enough practice, but he beat me at Ping-Pong. Surprisingly, after all his gloating and trash-talking, he didn't do much after he won.

"Twenty-one to twenty, I win," he said, smiling. "Good game."

"Do you want to play again?" I asked, still trying to think how to approach the subject of the prank.

"No," Allen said. "I'm reigning champ. I don't want to ruin my streak."

Then we played upstairs in Allen's toy room for a while. For months I had wanted to play with these toys, and now I couldn't enjoy them. Finally, I just blurted out what was on my mind.

"We can't play the trick on the Hagbarts."

"What?" Simon said, "Are you crazy? We've been planning this for weeks!"

"Yeah," said Allen, "and our plans are perfect! They're foolproof!"

"I don't think they deserve it," I said. "We've been just as mean to them as they were to us."

"Yeah, but they started it," Simon said. "We never would have done anything to them if they had left us alone. An 'eye for an eye.' That's in the Bible, you know."

"Well," I said, "it doesn't matter anymore. We just can't do it."

Simon and Allen sat staring at me, arms folded. I could tell they weren't convinced. So I told them everything, about how I got trapped hiding and how Gil's dad was mean to him. I was able to tell them without crying, but my voice was shaking by the time I was done.

"Are you sure it was his dad?" Simon asked, obviously shocked.

I realized I wasn't sure, but then remembered that Gil had called him "Dad" several times. I nodded.

Allen just sat there with his chin in his hand. He looked troubled.

Suddenly he stood up. "You know what we need to do?" he asked, and then without waiting for our answer, he got up and left the room.

We watched him leave, and then I turned to Simon. "So what do you think?"

Simon paused. "I don't think we should do it," he said finally. I nodded.

Allen came back in carrying the plans for the prank.

"These plans are perfect," he said solemnly. "They're foolproof. We can't let them fall into the wrong hands."

We nodded. It was kind of funny to see Allen being so dramatic, but I was glad he had come to the same conclusion we had. He looked at us seriously. "Follow me."

We followed him out to the backyard. His dad had an old metal barrel in the corner of the yard. It was blackened and full of snow and ash.

Allen solemnly struck a match on the metal edge of the barrel and then ceremoniously threw it and the envelope inside.

I laughed as we watched the plans shrivel up in the fire. Allen was a good friend.

Later that night at the Christmas Eve celebration, Allen told the Hagbarts that he wasn't going to help them. The Hagbarts were mad. I wondered if they would try to pick a fight, but since we were inside the gymnasium surrounded by adults, they couldn't do much but give us mean looks.

In my mind the fight was over, and so later that evening, when I went out in the hall to get a drink, I went alone.

I bent over for a drink, and somebody pushed my face into the water. I sputtered as I turned. It was Gil.

"Hi, Buck-Lee," he sneered. "Get a little wet?" He laughed at his own joke.

I wiped my face. "Hi, Gil," I said.

Gil didn't expect that reaction. He stared at me for a second, then sneered again. "I bet you asked for dolls for Christmas this year."

I was nervous, but managed to laugh a little. "Actually, we do every year. But since we want them as target practice, Mom and Dad never get them for us." Gil looked at me funny. Then he pushed my shoulder. "Well, you just wait until school again. We're going to give you some real trouble."

Suddenly there was a voice behind him. "Boys, that's enough." Brother Winston had turned the corner and stood with his arms folded, watching us.

Gil glared at Brother Winston. "What do you know? You're just an old man." He looked from Brother Winston's leathery old face to the tattoo on his forearm. "I gotta get back to my brothers," he mumbled and slunk back into the gymnasium.

Brother Winston looked at me for a moment. "How did everything turn out, Matthew?" he asked.

I didn't quite know what he was asking. Did he mean the little scuffle Gil and I had just had? Did he mean the whole fight with the bullies? Did he mean something else and I just couldn't think of it?

I thought for a moment and then said, "I think everything turned out okay."

Brother Winston looked at me, a smile playing on his lips. "All right then. You better get back inside. Have a merry Christmas."

"Merry Christmas," I replied and went back into the gymnasium to finish singing Christmas carols.

We left the celebration a little early so that we could drop off our last huge box of loot at the Hagbarts' house. There were games, toys, canned goods, and a ham that was as almost as big as John.

Since we knew they were still at the celebration, we didn't even bother knocking. I tried to imagine the look on their faces when they got home and found the food, toys, and goodies sitting on their porch. I reveled in the spirit of Christmas all the way home.

I was getting ready for bed when I had my last insight. Brother Winston had let me find out for myself what happened when a person seeks revenge. It seemed all year I had been having problems with the bullies. And we had gotten revenge several times. But none of it had brought me much happiness.

If I had done what I was supposed to in the beginning and just ignored the bullies, I could have possibly avoided all of this pain. Maybe the bullies would have just eventually left us alone. But it had seemed so important to get back at them. It had seemed important to find a way around the commandment that stood in our way.

But if I had just followed the commandments in the first place, I would have been better off.

"I wonder if it's like that with all of them," I wondered out loud.

"What are you talking about?" Simon asked from the top bunk.

"Nothing," I said.

Simon grinned. "Tomorrow is the big day!" he said excitedly.

I smiled and wiggled into my sheets. It was almost Christmas!

CHAPTER 22

I Guess It's All Sugar

"Matthew, wake up. It's Christmas."

I was instantly alert. "What time is it?" I asked. I wasn't even sure who I was talking to in the darkness.

"It's 2:30 in the morning," Simon replied.

"What?" I yelled. "We've slept in! I thought you had an internal clock."

"I do," Simon replied. "But I hit the snooze. Come on, let's get going."

We had drifted off to sleep around midnight, possibly later. We had played, talked, and laughed until Mom threatened to wait up for Santa and tell him not to leave anything. John, Peter, Jacob, Simon, and I ended up falling asleep in various positions around the room. Jacob was sucking his thumb on the end of my bed, probably still scared from the ghost stories we had told. John was sleeping horizontally on Simon's bed. Peter was on top of the rug, wrapped halfway by his blanket and still holding the army guy he had been playing with. Simon was propped against the bookcase, the book he had been reading now on the floor. I had taken all the pillows from the pillow fight and arranged them into a kind of soft couch in the corner.

We had all been asleep for over two hours now, and it was time to get cracking.

Mom and Dad had made the rule that nobody could get up to open presents until 6:00 A.M. on Christmas morning. Truth be told, they said 8:00, but it was an unwritten rule that you subtracted two hours. Simon had figured out a loophole a few years ago: we couldn't get up to open presents until 6:00 A.M., but since we weren't getting up to open presents, it was okay to get out of bed and search around.

Last year, Dad's youngest brother, Marc, had stayed over with us. He had slept out in the living room with the Christmas tree. We were a bit concerned because Uncle Marc had a beard. We thought he might scare off Santa, but then we remembered that Santa also had a beard, so it was all okay.

The only bad part was that Uncle Marc had booby-trapped the front room. When we tried to sneak out, we knocked over about fifteen pans that he had set out on a chair. The noise was enough to wake the dead and my parents. It scared us so bad we all ran back to the bedroom and just shook in our beds until we finally drifted off to sleep.

But this year nobody was out in the living room. As long as we were quiet, we could sneak out and survey the loot.

"Where are you going?" Peter asked. I could tell he was still half asleep.

"Santa came," Simon said. "We're going to see what—"

Peter was up from the rug in a flash. Simon had to grab ahold of his pajamas to keep him from running down the hall.

"We have to be very quiet," Simon whispered, "or we'll get sent back to bed."

We were halfway to the door when I stopped. "Let's get John," I said.

"Why?" Simon asked. But I was already shaking John awake.

"John," I said quietly, "wake up. We're going to see what Santa brought. Do you want to come?"

John woke up and looked at me. It took a moment for my words to register, but then his eyes brightened. "Sure!" he said.

We tiptoed out to the door, and then Simon gave us his lecture. "Okay, not a sound. If we get caught, we're in big trouble. Mom and Dad might not let us open any presents. Do you understand?"

We knew that would never happen, but it seemed like if we agreed, Simon would get started already.

"Hurry up!" Peter said, trying to edge past Simon.

"No, we can't hurry," Simon replied. "We have to go slow. Everybody step where I step. I've mastered where all the creaks are in the whole house."

I thought it was pretty silly, each of us slowly walking down the hall, stepping where Simon did, but sure enough, our creaky house was relatively quiet.

"I've been practicing this for weeks," Simon whispered, a bit of pride in his voice.

We got halfway down the hall, when Peter stopped before the bathroom door.

"Wait," Peter said. "I have to go to the bathroom."

Simon sighed. "Okay, but you have to be quiet, all right?"

Peter nodded.

"Step on the left-hand side when you get in, and then after two steps, move to the right. And not a sound, okay?"

Peter nodded again.

"And when you use the toilet . . . don't make noises."

"Can I go already?" Peter asked, and Simon nodded in the dark.

We had nothing to do but listen. Peter walked in and we didn't hear a sound. I tried to listen for any sound at all, but there was nothing. He had followed the instructions to the letter.

"He's pretty good," Simon said, impressed.

Then Peter flushed.

"WHOOPS!" Peter shouted from inside. "I didn't do that! I mean, I didn't mean to do that!"

Four boys tore down the stairs to the living room. We knew Mom or Dad would be in hot pursuit, so we had to move fast. John got the lights on before Dad hollered for everybody to get back in their beds. We dutifully obeyed, but not before we surveyed the beautiful scene before us. There were presents everywhere. Our stockings were bulging with toys and candy. I noticed that the cookies we had left out on a plate were half eaten. The old man had sat right there at our table and eaten our cookies and drunk our milk! Right there!

It was two hours before we all drifted back to sleep, but at 6:02, Simon was up again. We all galloped into Mom and Dad's room, jumping and yelling for them to wake up. Dad made a few jokes about being too tired and that he would get up in another four hours. We half dragged, half pushed them downstairs to eat breakfast.

If it were up to us, we would skip breakfast. Why should you worry about breakfast when there were loads of chocolate and candy in the next room? But it was another family rule. This rule, however, was tempered by the fact that Christmas was one of the few mornings a year when we got cold cereal. And where any other day of the year we would beg to pour our own bowl of cold cereal so we could get as much as possible, today we begged to pour our own so we could get as little as possible.

"You boys aren't going to skip breakfast and then fill up on sugar," Mom said, looking at our meager bowls. But then she smiled and sighed. "I guess it's all sugar. Just eat."

We shoved cold cereal down our throats and then ran to the front room. Some kids told me that on Christmas morning they just all grabbed presents and opened them. But at our house it was done in order. First we had a family prayer, and then Dad read us the Christmas story out of the Bible.

While family night was controlled chaos, this morning we were on our best behavior. To be sure, our excitement almost bubbled out our ears. But if we got rowdy, Dad would stop reading, and that pushed back the present-opening. So seven little kids sat there, arms folded, wiggling on the floor and couch in hopes that this would cause Dad to read faster.

When he was finally finished, Mom handed us each a big bowl and our stockings. This measure prevented some of the mess and kept our own candy together. We emptied our stockings into our bowls.

"Look what I got!" shouted Peter. "A taffy!"

"I got one too!" John yelled, holding his up.

Jacob was already eating his, and the twins were drooling colored drool, something they would do all morning.

"A race car!" Peter shouted. "Matthew, did you get a race car?"

"Yep!" I shouted. "Mine is red. What color is yours?"

"It's blue! I'm so happy it's blue! It's my favorite color for race cars!"

And then the morning only got more intense as Dad handed out the presents, one by one. We would each end up with about seven or eight presents, some of them big, some of them small. But when you have seven kids opening seven presents, Christmas morning is stretched out to about three hours. We got some from Mom and Dad, some from Santa Claus, and some from Mrs. Claus. We never really liked the ones from Mrs. Claus. She gave things like socks and underwear.

As we got more and more of what we'd wanted, or when we got things and then told everybody it was what we'd wanted, the excitement kept building and building. I got a Stretch Armstrong, something I had begged my parents to get me for six months. Simon got a chemistry set and several books. Peter got a large GI Joe vehicle that we all drooled over. And, of course, we all got Legos.

We thought of our new toys, we thought of the whole week we would have to play with them, and pretty soon we were yelling and shouting at the top of our lungs every time somebody opened anything, even when the gifts ended up being "practical."

"Look at what I got!" Peter shouted after opening up a large box.

"What is it?" I asked. From his excited tone it must have been something good.

"I don't know!" Peter yelled. "But I love it!"

"It's food storage," Mom said. "That's enough Cream of Wheat to keep you full for six months."

"I love Cream of Wheat!" Peter shouted. "And don't worry, I'll share it with everybody."

"You're too kind," Dad said, rolling his eyes.

Finally the presents were all gone. We had given our little homemade things to Mom and Dad, and we had given our presents to our brothers. We each had our own piles of things that made our hearts beat faster just looking at them. The morning was just winding down when Dad pulled out an envelope with a bow on it.

"Looks like there is one more thing," he said. "This is from Mom and Dad to the entire family. Who wants to open it?"

Normally this would have caused a fight, but it was Christmas, so we were all feeling nice. Peter was chosen to open it.

He opened it up, but there was just a piece of paper in it.

"What does it say?" Simon asked.

Peter slowly sounded out each word.

"Dear kids. This present isn't something you can play with right now. You'll have to wait seven more months. Love, Mom and Dad."

Simon started whooping and throwing bits of tinsel in the air. It took me a bit longer to get it, but then I joined him, throwing every piece of wrapping paper I could find. Peter and John thought it was funny and started pelting each other with balls of wrapping paper. Jacob scrunched up his taffy wrappers and threw them as well. Mom and Dad just watched, laughing at our excitement. Even the twins were laughing whenever they got conked by a wrapping-paper ball or whenever a glittery string settled into their hair.

"What does it mean?" John asked through all the commotion.

"It means we get a new brother!" I shouted.

"Or a sister," Mom piped up.

"You guys don't know how to have girls," Simon said, laughing, and Dad joined in.

Christmas morning was over, and we'd eventually have to go back to school. But we had a whole week of vacation left, and I knew our family would make the most of it.

EPILOGUE

When we went back to school after Christmas break, the Hagbarts were gone. I found out from Mom, much later, that they had moved in with their grandmother, who lived near Bear Lake. I guess it was a better situation for them.

I felt a bit empty. On the one hand, I was happy the Hagbarts were gone—no more bully problems. On the other hand, the Hagbarts had taken up so much of my attention that I didn't quite know what to do with them gone. However, with the new baby coming, school, and my dad's new calling as Scoutmaster, I soon moved on to other adventures.

The Hagbarts left an impression on us in more ways than one. That next summer, when we took our annual trip to Bear Lake, there, much to my surprise, was our crazy sand art project—"Bob." It had somehow survived the winter. The face was the same, and underneath we could still read our names. But there were also a lot of changes. Somebody had cleaned all of the little furrows, and now there was a Mrs. Bob who had crazy lightning hair, as well as a few strange-looking children who looked more like mutant frogs than humans. A few other kids had signed their names under ours. It was no longer our project; it was a community project. And it was cool.

But what surprised me the most was that there, under the whole project, was another message. It read, "Don't mess with this, or you'll have to answer to the Hagbarts. And we rule this beach!"

My first thought was that the Hagbarts hadn't changed all that much. Even in a sand message they were trying to be intimidating.

But then again, they knew we had made Bob, and they hadn't destroyed it. In fact, I imagined that they had made some of the additions. I smiled. In a small way, we were still linked. I truly hoped they would be happy in life. I knew, as I ran to play with my brothers, that I was. And everybody deserves that.

ABOUT THE AUTHOR

Matthew Buckley grew up in Riverside, Utah, and is the second oldest of ten boys and one girl. To date he has has five sons of his own.

Matthew graduated from Utah State University with degrees in political science and instructional technology. He currently works for the university as director of the USU OpenCourseWare project. In his spare time, Matthew likes to attend game night, cook for his family, and liberate information.

Matthew would love to hear from any of his readers. Please write to him at info@covenant-lds.com, or visit his blog at http://chickenarmpits.blogspot.com.

Matthew Buckley is the pen name of Marion Jensen. But don't hold that against either of them.